THE
BARLOWS

ALSO BY JOANNE DEMAIO

The Seaside Saga

Blue Jeans and Coffee Beans
The Denim Blue Sea
Beach Blues
Beach Breeze
The Beach Inn
Beach Bliss
Castaway Cottage
Night Beach
Little Beach Bungalow
Every Summer
Salt Air Secrets
Stony Point Summer
The Beachgoers
Shore Road
The Wait
The Goodbye
The Barlows
The Visitor
—And More Seaside Saga Books—

ALSO BY JOANNE DEMAIO

Beach Cottage Series

The Beach Cottage
Back to the Beach Cottage

Standalone Novels

True Blend
Whole Latte Life

The Winter Series

Snowflakes and Coffee Cakes
Snow Deer and Cocoa Cheer
Cardinal Cabin
First Flurries
Eighteen Winters
Winter House
—And More Winter Books—

the barlows

BOOK 17

JOANNE DEMAIO

one

LISTEN.

The sea demands it. Demands that you pay attention to it.

That you sense it.

Hear it.

Acknowledge it.

Watch it.

Heed it.

Jason Barlow's learned this by living beside the sea. It's always—*always*—telling you something. Often that mighty sea is telling you what's *about* to happen. With its changing color, or wavelets rippling the surface, or ominous incoming swells, it's making you aware of something coming. Something sinister, maybe—a nasty storm, or a school of minnows being chased down by aggressive bluefish on the hunt.

Yes, Jason knows. If you just pay attention, the sea gives you fair warning.

So does life. That much he's learned—the hard way. By *not* paying attention.

Because how many times has an unexpected split second turned the tide in his life? How often has he been a heartbeat away from everything changing? A breath away from disaster. Around the corner from rippling trouble. A moment away from swells of darkness.

Oh, Jason Barlow knows that feeling too damn well.

Knows the instant whirlwind of tragedy descending on two brothers on a motorcycle one hot August day a decade ago.

Knows what would've happened if one more second had passed before he wrenched an inebriated Kyle to safety on the boardwalk three years ago. Kyle would've suffered a fatal fall, plunging twenty feet to sand-coated concrete. He wouldn't be here today.

Jason also knows that if his own father was moments sooner lining up to trek through a jungle in 'Nam, that godawful day would've been the end. The Viet Cong's punji-stick trap would've impaled his father, rather than the comrade ahead of him.

There's more, too.

Jason knows that a desperate hour ten years ago—when he'd hit rock bottom—was the hour his father hauled him out onto Stony Point Beach. The hour he got Jason to walk again, damn it. "Last chance. Walk or get out of here," his father ordered. "Out of my home. Out of my life," he added, his voice catching on the words. Moments later, when Jason lifted one foot, then his new prosthetic foot, his father fought tears. He stood beside Jason—and they slowly crossed the beach together.

2

Jason knows, too, that a minute's hesitation, a mere change of mind, would've kept him out of the airport one night three years ago. A summer night when he found Maris and her packed duffel at that airport. When his words pleaded with her. When he whispered, "*Don't go, Maris. Don't leave me.*"

Minutes, moments, seconds, flashes, breaths when his world changed. Was tipped on its axis. Was pulled out from under him when he least expected it.

Times when one or another of the Barlows was in some sort of purgatory, and life—Jason's, Neil's, or his father's—was either decimated by the impurities of the world, or cleansed of them.

But finally—*finally*—the seas of Jason's life calmed.

These past couple of weeks, the waters parted and someone above said, *This guy is cleared. All's good. Here it is, man. Happiness. Take it. Relish it. Hold onto it.*

Maris was back in his life. In his every day.

Hell, they just finished up dinner at the local pizza place. At a window table overlooking the bay, they ate. Leaned in close and talked—just like old times. She told him about her day. He told her that he'd be doing some Friday night fishing with the guys. But first, Maris had to drop her car off at the dealer.

Which is where they're headed now. In his SUV, he's been following behind her as she drives along the rural road. It's the twilight hour of this mid-September day. On the lightly wooded street, the golden sun is low; shadows, long.

Peaceful.

Ordinary. Easy.

And now—this.

Again. It's happening again.

The tide's turning in his life—with fair warning—just like the sea.

Jason sees it, that fair warning.

And he damn well knows to pay attention. To be on high alert.

There.

Up ahead, a motion catching his eye can take everything away.

There's a deer in a grassy area off to the right. The animal isn't grazing, but is a flash of tawny movement as it bounds into the street. Thankfully, Maris sees the deer. To Jason's relief, her brake lights briefly flicker. So he knows she's watching that deer leap past while she's driving.

But Maris must be watching only that *fleeing* deer—off to her left now.

Because she's *not* braking for the next deer on her right. No red taillights come on as that second deer runs out of a stand of trees.

"Shit, *shit!*" Jason says aloud in his vehicle. He almost missed it, too. "To your *right*, Maris! Look! There's another one!"

Everything's a flash, then. A blur that happens in only seconds.

And in those seconds, he knows. Maris' attention is on the first deer. *Not* the second one coming up behind it.

Not until it's too late.

Jason can't miss that it's too late—and there's *nothing* he can do.

Maris doesn't notice that second deer leaping into the street until the animal's right in front of her moving car.

She swerves and slams on the brakes.

Hard.

Hard enough for those damn brake lights to come on—steady now. Steady and veering from side to side as her car fishtails across the road. A sound comes, too. It's her locked tires squealing over the pavement.

"*No, no, no, no,*" Jason whispers, watching it all go down. "*Maris.*"

He grips his steering wheel and slows up. And leans forward to watch closely through his windshield—as if he can steer Maris out of this. Can somehow help her.

Instead, *helpless*, Jason only sees it all.

Sees the very last rays of sunlight glimmer on the metal of Maris' skidding car.

Sees her car spinning sideways now.

The tires screeching.

The deer mid-leap—its white tail flashing.

A blur of red brake lights and out-of-control car weaving on the twilight's gray pavement.

Motion, motion.

It's a moment in Jason's life—another precarious moment—that can go either way.

A moment in which control is recovered or lost.

Which spins into darkness or light.

Gratitude or grief.

Again.

"*God, no,*" Jason whispers, urgently pulling his SUV to the side of the road.

two

"WHERE THE HELL IS JASON?" Kyle asks. He's leaning against a boulder as the sun sets. There's a cell phone in his hand, too, that he scrolls for any messages. Any voicemails. "Nothing."

"Give him time," Matt says from his fishing perch on the rocks. "It's a long haul to the car dealer and back."

"Let me try him again." Kyle's still leaning as his thumbs fly over the phone. "*Get a move on, guy,*" he whispers while texting. "*Moon's full, fish'll be biting.*" After finally pocketing his phone, Kyle looks out over Long Island Sound. That big, low moon drops a swath of gold across the water.

"Still no word?" Cliff asks from the rocks below, at the water's edge.

"Zilch," Kyle tells him.

"That's odd." Cliff turns and casts his fishing line. "Well, let's see if I can catch anything before he shows, or if the whole night's a bust—like everything else lately."

Cliff's standing near a tide pool, where the salty water swirls among the seaweed-covered rocks.

"Lighten up, Judge. You oughta snag *something*. Because that there's the harvest moon," Kyle explains as he baits his hook. "So named because back in olden times, that September moon gave farmers a few extra hours of good light to harvest their crops." Kyle casts his line whizzing out over the water. "So we should be able to harvest something, too. Something *aquatic* ... beneath that epic moonlight. Hook a few fish."

They're quiet then, the three of them. Matt moves to a new spot further out on the rocks. Cliff reels in his line some. And Kyle turns to scan the nearby stretch of sand. "*Sheesh*, you'd think a spotlight's on the beach, the way that moon's lighting it up." He bends a little and squints into the night. "No sign of Barlow headed this way with his dog, though."

"*Hey*," Matt calls out, keeping his voice low. "*Any nibbles yet?*"

"Nothing, dude," Kyle says, glancing at his own slack fishing line. In the swath of moonlight, his bobber idly floats on the rippling water. "Damn, it looks almost like daytime," he remarks. "Not sure I've ever seen a full moon as brilliant as that one." He moves to a nearby boulder, leans against it and further contemplates the lunar view. "Wonder if any farmers are out tonight," Kyle muses. "Toiling in the fields. Gathering corn. Bet it'd be a sweet sight to see. All those corn tassels looking wispy and golden across the night field. That big ol' orb of a moon dropping illumination across the earth."

"Would you shut up, Bradford?" Cliff calls over his

shoulder, then swigs from the beer can he holds. "Going on and on about that *ridiculous* moon. You think any of us are farmers here?"

"What?" Kyle starts reeling in his fishless line. "What's your problem?"

Cliff hesitates for a long moment before setting his beer on a boulder-top. "You really want to know?" he finally asks, turning to Kyle.

"Yeah," Kyle says. "You bet I do."

"I want to know, too," Matt pipes in from his fishing spot. "You've had a chip on your shoulder all week on our morning workouts, Cliff. Could barely talk to you."

"Fine." Cliff glares over at Matt, then tugs on his line when it goes taut. "Fine, I'll tell you." Cliff reels in more line—which some fish takes right back out. "*You're* my problem, Kyle. And seriously? It's about all I can do not to give you a shiner the *size* of that blessed harvest moon."

"*Me?* Wait, *I'm* your problem?" Kyle asks, hitting himself in the chest. "Did I miss something? What gives, Commish?"

Cliff throws Kyle another look over his shoulder, then glances at Matt working his way closer across the rocks. "I'll tell both of you what gives, all right?" Cliff relents. "But it doesn't go beyond these rocks here. Got it?"

"What do you mean?" Matt asks, heading now for the cooler Kyle brought.

"Means what I'm about to say is *not* public knowledge. Not meant to go further than right here. So raise a beer can in solidarity—or forget it." As he says it, Cliff reaches for his own can on that nearby boulder and lifts the can to the night sky.

But Kyle just finishes reeling in his slack fishing line, sets down the rod and folds his arms across his chest. Eyes Cliff, too, until Matt nudges him and gives him a can of beer from that cooler. So Kyle does it. He snaps open the beer, takes a long swig, then raises the can right up to that rising orb of a moon.

"Okay, a toast is as good as your word." When Cliff's fishing line goes slack, he sets down the rod. "And it's not *really* your fault I've got a problem, Kyle," Cliff admits. "But hell, you're an easy enough target." Cliff climbs over a few rocks toward them as he explains. "You see, a week ago, I was about to propose to Elsa. I mean it was *imminent*. Only minutes away. Had it all planned out."

"What?" Kyle asks. "For real?"

"It's true," Cliff assures him, holding his index finger and thumb spaced just so. "Came *this* close, I tell you."

"Way to go, Cliff," Matt yells over. "And about time!"

Kyle squints through the moonlit shadows at Cliff. "So what's that have to do with *me*?"

"This." Cliff takes a long breath. Looks at the moon, then back at the guys. "On my big day, I got dressed to the nines ... took my lady out on the town for a night of music and dancing ... and was going to *propose*," he quietly reveals, "beneath the stars at the bandshell concert."

Kyle's eyes briefly drop closed. "*Gesù, Santa Maria.* I had no idea."

"Oh, *that* was obvious." Cliff finishes the last of his beer and deposits the empty can in the cooler. "The way you and Lauren planted yourselves on that picnic blanket beside me and Elsa. And could you have stayed *any* longer? I mean, the whole damn night—just *parked* there. I sure as heck wasn't going to pop the question with an audience."

"Well, why didn't you pull me aside?" Kyle asks as he opens the cooler and lifts a container of sliced salami, crackers and cubed cheese. "*Say* something," he insists, topping a cracker with the meat and cheese.

"Like what? Kick you and Lauren out? Elsa would've yelled at me if I did, so the night was doomed either way." Cliff waves them off then. Turning, he retrieves his fishing rod from the lower rocks. "Look, Kyle," he says, picking up his fishing gear. "Sorry about what I said before. No hard feelings?"

"Nah," Kyle tells him around a mouthful of his salami-cracker concoction. "I get it. You're just down in the dumps now."

"And listen, Cliff." Matt pauses and takes the food container from Kyle, then puts a hunk of cheese on his own cracker. "You hang in there with Elsa. It ain't over till it's over," he says, biting into that cracker. "So just, you know … try again."

"Eh." Cliff hauls his fishing pole and small tackle box over the rocks. Silently, he wanders toward the beach. "I'm done fishing, fellas. *Done with everything.*"

"Wait, Judge!" Kyle calls out. "You want some of this food I brought?"

"Drown your sorrows in salami, cheese and crackers?" Matt yells to him.

"It's pepper jack cheese," Kyle adds.

Which gets Cliff to turn back. He reaches into the plastic tub, scoops a handful of the appetizer—little bit of this, some of that—and heads off the rocks.

"Guy's in rough shape," Matt says, assembling his own deluxe salami-cracker sandwich now.

"Yeah. Dejected with a capital D." Kyle glances at Cliff departing, then shrugs. "Well ... more food for Nick this way—whenever he gets off his shift. Barlow, too. Speaking of which," Kyle says, pulling out his cell phone, "let me text Jason again." He squints at his phone and whispers the typed words. "*Got some good grub here. Where the hell you at?*"

three

QUICK, QUICK. HE'S GOT TO move fast.

Jason *has* to get out of his SUV. He has to get to Maris in case she needs help. In case her skidding car veers off the road and into a tree. In case she's hurt. Or in case she *can't* get out. Or is in any danger.

It's all going down in seconds. Blurring seconds. All at once.

Without taking his eyes off Maris' wayward car, Jason steers his SUV onto the road's shoulder. It's a narrow lane, partially paved, partially graveled. On this rural street, some wild brush and grasses encroach on the shoulder, too. His vehicle's tires spin over the grit.

But as soon as he parks and opens his door, things change. There's a shift.

A difference.

He can't miss it. Ahead of him in the dusky twilight, the red brake lights on Maris' swerving car flicker, then go off.

Yes. Good, Maris. Good, Jason thinks—still watching. She maneuvers her car out of its skid. Somewhat straightens the vehicle on the road, then manages to *also* pull onto the shoulder. The car lurches over a few pavement heaves and keeps going—not stopping until half off the shoulder, half on the abutting scrubby grasses.

Then? Nothing. Nothing for a long second.

Until her car door *flies* open and Maris bolts out of the vehicle. Standing there, she turns this way, then that—her long black tank-top dress coiling around her legs, the low twist of her brown hair falling loose. Her eyes are panicked as she searches for him. Finally, her denim vest hanging open over her dress, she trots roadside straight to him. Straight into his arms as he meets up with her.

"Maris!" he says, feeling her barrel right into his body—getting him to step back with the force. Her grip is tight; her breathing, fast. He feels it all.

"*Jason!* Oh my God, Jason!" she sobs. "That *deer,* I didn't see it. Didn't realize there were *two!*"

"*I know. I know.*" As he whispers, his hands cradle her head on his shoulder. And they keep moving, his hands. Keep calming. Keep reassuring, the way one hand won't let up holding her head to him, the other hand stroking her fallen hair—over and over and over again. From the top of her head, down her back, again. "*Shh. Shh,*" he murmurs into her ear. "*You're okay, sweetheart.*"

Shudders. While holding her roadside, that's all Jason feels—Maris' body shuddering. So he leans back a little and tries to see her eyes. Her beautiful eyes. But she's sobbing now, into his neck, his shoulder. Close, standing so close. Nothing can come between them.

And when he finally manages to tip her head up—lift her face to his—her eyes are closed. Her face, drawn. The realization of what *nearly* happened has overcome her.

"Maris," he says, kissing away some of the tears, then pressing her head to his shoulder again. Standing there on the scrubby grass, he just buries his face in her neck. Another shake shudders her body, so he doesn't let her out of the hug. "*Shh, shh.* You're okay," Jason's low voice tells her.

"*The deer,*" she finally gets out, glancing over toward her car. "Did I—"

"The deer's fine. You didn't hit it." He scans the other side of the winding, country road. "There," he says, pointing to both deer safely grazing in a clearing near the trees.

When Maris looks past him to the foraging deer, Jason looks with her. The two deer stand there, heads lowered, serene as can be. Unscathed. Oblivious to the catastrophic threat they'd just escaped.

Maris turns to him, wipes her face and fights another sob. "*Jason,*" she whispers. "The way it just happened. I didn't know …"

"*Hey, come here.*" Jason quietly embraces her again. Holds her head to his shoulder. Holds her for all he's worth, actually. He doesn't push her to go on, to finish her dangling thought. He just keeps his arms wrapped around her body pressed to his.

Occasional vehicles pass. Their tires hum across the pavement; their headlights shine. A warm wind kicks up with each car's movement. That wind reaches them standing there in the scrubby roadside grasses. The sun has gone down now, too. In its place, a full moon is just cresting the treetops.

Holding Maris in his arms still, Jason sees it all. That low moon, massive and pale. It casts dappled light on the wooded stretch of road. On a deserted country barn ahead. On the two deer lingering in the shadows. On Maris' car driven right off the road's shoulder.

four

IT DOESN'T TAKE MUCH.

Doesn't take much to fatigue you. To quiet you. To debilitate you. To scare the God damn daylights out of you. Not much. Just your life put in peril in such a way that the potential is there—the potential to lose *everything* you love. Lose it all.

Jason knows this. Knows it personally.

He knows something else, too. Knows the antidote for when this happens.

It's home. *Get home.*

So in the evening shadows thirty minutes later, he's driving his SUV beneath the stone trestle into Stony Point. Maris sits beside him in the passenger seat. She hasn't said much. And she wouldn't. She really needs the antidote. Few words have come on the drive along the winding roads here. There have been only some hushed exclamations as Maris pictures that deer leaping in her path. A quiet gasp as she quells a sudden sob. Jason reaching over and squeezing her hand.

Finally, they're passing beneath the dark stone tunnel and stopping at the guard post.

"Hey, *hey*. It's the Barlows," Nick calls over his shoulder while holding paint chips to the guard shack walls. He pockets the chips and crosses the street to Jason's open window.

"Nick," Jason answers with a slight nod.

"Getting ready to fish, man?" Nick asks, glancing at his watch. "Just about to clock off my shift. You coming?"

"Not tonight."

"What? Why not?" As Nick asks, he leans in and sees Maris.

Jason glances at her, too. She's still teary; her face is drawn; her hair, tucked back.

"*Whoa*, Maris," Nick remarks.

Maris manages only a small smile. "Almost got in a really bad accident, Nick," she tells him.

"Oh my God," Nick says, gripping the door at the open window and squinting through the evening light. "Are you all right?"

"She is," Jason tells him, his voice quiet. "Just shook up."

Nick looks from Maris to Jason. "What happened, guys?"

Jason gives the condensed version—because he knows. After the night's frightening turn, Maris needs that antidote. Needs to quickly get home.

"I'm fine, really," Maris says now. She leans across the front seat toward the window where Nick stands. "Just want to go home. I'm pretty tired."

"Totally get it." Nick's backing up as Jason puts the

SUV in gear. "Well, hey," Nick adds, managing to slap Jason's arm through the window. "I'm *so* relieved you're both okay. That deer, too?"

"Safe and grazing on the other side of the street." Jason gets the SUV slowly rolling then. "But a close call for sure," he says to Nick through the window.

As they drive away, Nick gives a wave—but suddenly motions to them. "Wait! Anything I can do for you?" he calls out.

"Yeah." Jason briefly stops, leans out and calls back. "Tell the guys I'm bailing on fishing, would you?"

Kyle doesn't have to check his watch. He knows Jason's late by the moon itself. It's rising higher in the night sky. The golden light it drops spreads wider and wider across the dark, rippling water. The beach is illuminated by that moonlight, too. And there's no sign of Jason—fishing pole slung over his shoulder—crossing the sand. Only Nick is approaching. He's got on his fishing vest, each pocket stuffed with lures and hooks and extra fishing line.

"Yo, Nick!" Matt calls out from the rock jetty.

Kyle waves to Nick, too, then gives his phone one last check.

"Nothing. I give up," Kyle says, pocketing his phone. "Barlow's AWOL."

"Not AWOL," Nick lets on as he climbs over the rocks. "Just saw him at the trestle."

"*Finally.*" Kyle picks up his fishing rod and maneuvers past a couple of boulders while scoping out the water. "He shouldn't be too much longer, then."

"Well … not sure about that," Nick says, still making his way to them.

"What do you mean?" Matt asks. He's standing further out on the rocks and tugging on his slack fishing line.

"Change of plans tonight," Nick explains. He sets down his fishing gear, unhitches his rod from the rod-and-reel holding loops on his vest, then sets the rod aside.

"Come on, spill it already," Kyle tells him. "What's the deal with Barlow?"

"Not Jason. But Maris. Nearly cracked up her car."

"*What?*" Kyle asks.

"No way!" Matt calls over. "She all right?"

Nick nods. "She is."

"Thank *God*," Kyle says to the skies over the sea. "But shit, what happened?"

"From what I can gather, they were bringing her car in for service and some deer spooked her. Jumped in the road right in front of her," Nick goes on. "Guess Maris almost lost control of the vehicle."

"Wow, I'll have to let Eva know," Matt says.

"Oh, man." Kyle tips up the brim of his *Gone Fishing* cap and casts his line. "Must've shook Maris up some."

Nick gives another nod. "It did. She went into a nasty skid, but got out of it okay."

"Still, that sucks," Matt calls over from his fishing spot.

"Poor Maris." Kyle gives a *tsk* and slow shake of his head.

"Luckily, Jason was right behind her in his SUV. So they're good now." Nick pulls a few lures from his vest pocket before looking out over the rocks. "And hey, where's my boss tonight anyway?"

"Cliff? He was here before, but hit the road," Matt tells him, right as his reel spins out with a fresh catch on the line.

"Maybe this full moon's bringing bad luck. Barlows almost cracking up the car, and the commish in a sour mood. Said he wasn't much feeling fishing tonight," Kyle adds. "Why? Need something from the boss, Nicholas?"

Nick's pulling several swatches out of that multitude of pockets on his fishing vest. "Been checking paint colors in the evening light," he explains. "For the guard shack. Cliff wanted my vote so he could buy the paint tomorrow."

"You pick one?" Kyle asks, leaning against his boulder now while waiting for a fish nibble.

"Eh. I'm between two." Nick fans out the samples in his hand. "Could use your input."

"All right," Matt says. "Hold them up. Get your mini flashlight on them, too."

"Yeah," Kyle adds. "From your vest pocket."

"Okay, here goes," Nick tells them while shining the flashlight beam on two paint samples. "Quick. Go with your gut. In three seconds, point to the color you'd pick." He raises a silvery-gray and a navy-blue chip high in the air. "And—three. Two. *One.*"

They both point to the navy chip.

"Darn it!" Nick turns the paint chips and studies them. "I was leaning toward the other one."

"Gray?" Matt asks.

"No, it's *silver*," Nick clarifies. "Like, you know, a seagull feather? A little brighter than gray."

"But nothing's more coastal than navy," Kyle counters. "With nice white trim."

"I quit." Nick pockets his mini flashlight and paint swatches and heads toward the food cooler.

Kyle gives a shrug. "So where's Barlow now?" he calls back to him.

"Home," Nick answers.

Kyle squints over at him. "That right?"

"Yep. He's home with Maris. Guess he's got stuff to take care of with the car and all. Said to tell you he's bailing on fishing tonight."

"Yeah. Me, too," Kyle says while reeling in his line. "I'm outta here, guys."

"What?" Matt's making his way down the rocks toward the water while still reeling in some fighting fish. "Where *you* going now?"

"The Barlows'." Kyle resettles his cap on his head and leans his fishing rod on his shoulder. "Want to check on them."

"Well, text us if they need anything," Matt manages to yell as he nets his struggling fish.

"Hold up!" Nick calls, too. "What about your cooler? What's on the menu tonight?"

"Salami, sliced cheese and crackers." Waving them off, Kyle heads toward his pickup parked at the end of Champion Road. "You guys finish the chow," he calls back. "And drop off the cooler at my place afterward."

Jason closes the window near the sofa. "Better?" he asks Maris.

"Yeah. I felt a little chilly." Maris shifts where she sits

on the couch. She's still in her long black tank-top dress, but wears a sweater now. Her legs are up on the couch cushions, and she's fluffing a pillow behind her.

So as she gets comfortable, Jason sets the living room lamp on dim before lifting a knitted throw off the back of the couch. He drapes the blanket over her. "This'll help you warm up," he says, tucking the soft fabric around her legs. Maddy's been pacing the living room, too. The dog's picked up on Maris' distress—enough to jump right on the end of the sofa, squeeze in past Maris' feet and cautiously curl up on the cushion.

"Maddy!" Maris begins to scold.

But Jason stops her. "Let her stay," he says before turning to the German shepherd and scratching her ears. "But *just* tonight," he adds in a stern voice. He stifles a smile, too, as the guilty dog slinks her head down low at his tone.

There's a noise, then, right as Jason's getting the TV remote for Maris. Tires squeal when a vehicle speeds up the long driveway running alongside the house. Seconds later, they hear someone coming up the back deck stairs. The slider scrapes open, too.

Jason reaches for Maddy growling and shifting on the couch. "No. No, girl." He grabs hold of her collar and tells her, "*Quiet.*"

"Yo, Barlows! What's going on?" Kyle's voice calls out.

"Stay put with the dog," Jason tells Maris when she starts to get up. He pats the blanket and keeps them settled on the couch. "I'll go see Kyle, fill him in some."

When Jason gets to the kitchen, Kyle's just closing up the slider.

"Kyle," Jason says. "Let yourself in, why don't you?"

"Thanks." Kyle turns back to Jason. "Had to, after what I just heard."

And Jason knows right away from whom. Because Kyle's got on not only a denim jacket over a green tee and gray jeans, but the dead giveaway? The *Gone Fishing* cap he wears. Not to mention, his battered leather hiking shoes are wet from fishing on the rocks. "You must've talked to Nick."

"Shit, yeah. He told me Maris practically totaled her car?"

"Totaled? Wasn't *that* bad. More a near miss between her car and a deer. Maris swerved and the car went into a good skid before—"

"She all right?" Kyle interrupts, looking past Jason. "Where is she? I texted Lauren and she wondered if you got Maris checked out at the hospital?"

"What? No, it wasn't like that." Jason walks to the counter and squeezes out a teabag steeping in Maris' favorite porcelain cup. "She's fine and in the living room, guy." He adds a touch of cream to the tea and gently stirs it all. "Here, bring her this. She'd like to see you," Jason tells him as he hands Kyle the teacup.

"First off," Kyle says over his shoulder as he carries the tea past the new denim-blue island and its gray-and-white swirled top. "*Sweet* reno here. What a kitchen going on now."

"Thanks, man. It was all Maris' doing." Jason hitches his head for Kyle to get that tea to her, then follows behind. In the hallway, he hears Maris talking to her sister on the phone. "No, *no*. I'm really *fine*, Eva," she's insisting. "Just tired. Come see me tomorrow, okay?" When Maris spots Kyle bringing her the tea, she ends the call and turns to him.

"Hey, Maris," Kyle's saying while crossing the living room—right as Maddy jumps off the couch and hurries to him. "Good to see you here ... and *not* in some emergency room."

"Oh, Kyle. Yeah, I'm pretty glad, too," Maris agrees from where she's still sitting beneath her blanket.

Jason leans in the doorway and just watches.

"You feeling okay?" Kyle asks, lowering that teacup to her.

"I am."

But when Maris reaches for her tea, Jason sees it—the telltale sign that says otherwise. That says she's *not* really okay. Her hands tremble.

Maris gives Kyle a quick smile and motions to the coffee table. "Can you just put the tea there?" she asks.

"Oh, sure. Sure." Kyle sets down the cup, but doesn't stop with that. He also bends and gives Maris a good, long hug. "Thank *God* you're home, safe and sound," he says into the hug. "Stopped my heart for a second there."

To that, Maris squeezes his shoulder.

When Kyle straightens, he pats Maddy at his feet before turning to Jason in the doorway. "Listen, must've been a scary night. You need anything, guy? Some help around here?"

"Matter of fact, I do." Jason motions for Kyle to follow him. "Need you to ride shotgun."

five

MAYBE A CHANGE OF SCENERY will help.

Elsa thinks this as she settles with a glass of wine in the old Foley's back room Friday night. Because the past few days haven't been easy. Cliff saw the flowers from Mitch— a bouquet of wild beach roses and sunflower blossoms, all tucked in with larkspur and blades of dune grasses. Oh, Cliff didn't say anything when he picked them up off her front stoop, but some things a woman knows. And Elsa *knows* Cliff would've read the card tucked into that arrangement. Elsa reaches now to the vase on the booth table and touches a fading rose. Then Cliff went and shut down her tomato cart. Well. *Technically*, the BOG shut it down. Cliff just taped up her cute little cart like it was a crime scene. Sadly, then, she dismantled the cart— tomatoes and cashbox and striped sun umbrella and all.

Then there's Celia. The friction between them isn't right. But Elsa gets it. Instead of going forward with the inn's opening two weeks ago, she kept it closed without consulting Celia—her assistant innkeeper. Didn't so much as ask her opinion. *And* left Celia adrift with no work.

So sitting alone in the back room now feels like a mini getaway from her troubles. Jason certainly knew what he was doing when he insisted on preserving the room's history during the inn's renovation. His vision created a nostalgic ambiance—a time travel of sorts. The vintage pinball machine glimmers in the corner. A large, empty picture frame hangs where that fabled moose head once did. September's salty air drifts off the distant beach and right into the open sliding windows. The jukebox quietly plays a few summertime songs. Familiar tunes about warm, sultry nights. And longings. And easy living. Outside on the deck, paper lanterns glow in the night. If she looks just right, can't Elsa see vague silhouettes slow-dancing in the evening shadows around her? Can't she visualize those epic stories she's heard about this room. Lovelorn ghosts of the past still hanging around.

Elsa sighs then. It's simply that kind of night. But she quickly shakes off the ghosts and shadows. Tugs close the white crochet topper she'd put on over her black sheath tank top and faded skinny jeans. Her laptop is open on the table in her booth, and she figures she'll catch up on her emails. While doing so, she also dips a biscotti into her wine and takes a sweet bite. Her eyes drop closed for a long moment as she just listens to the jukebox's sentimental song. Breathes that salt air that cures what ails you.

And she knows precisely what's ailing *her* these days. Life, itself.

Maybe Concetta will have some answers for her.

Which gets Elsa to finally open the new email from her friend across the Atlantic.

But what comes as a surprise is the *seriousness* of Concetta's words. So serious, it has Elsa scroll down to reread the email *she'd* sent to her friend only yesterday.

Concetta, you are a wise woman, Elsa had written. *Being on the outside and looking in, you have clarity. So can you offer me any advice? Because lately? It seems every move I make—whether with Cliff, or Mitch, or even Celia—is the wrong one.*

Concetta, as usual, gets right to the heart of the matter. There are no minced words for Elsa. Only the clear truth.

Do not let one more day go by without reaching out to Celia, Concetta warns. *Your famiglia is everything. Your beautiful granddaughter, Aria, is so much of your world.*

Elsa pauses and looks out the window beside her. The night is quiet. Those paper lanterns shimmer in the mist. Well, maybe they shimmer a little in the mist, and a little from behind her sudden tears. She dabs at them, then reads the rest of Concetta's message. Reads the phrases *urging* Elsa to work on things with Celia—right away. There are no funny quips in the message. No lighthearted remarks— as though Concetta knows; as though sad mistakes of her own have taught her wisely.

If you fix things with Celia first, the email concludes, *you'll have clarity on the rest.*

Oh, how Elsa misses Concetta. Her dear friend always reminds her of what she already—somehow—knows.

Now Elsa lifts her hands to the keyboard and writes back, sending her words across the ocean and straight to Concetta's villa in Milan.

You're very right, Elsa's fingers type in the softly lit back

27

room. *It's too late to start up with Celia this evening. But I'm very bothered by Cliff shutting down my tomato cart—or by the way he actually handled it. So I'm going to see him tonight, and will see Celia in the morning. Promise.*

Talk soon, my friend.

⌒

It's quiet in the trailer.

So quiet that Cliff just sits at his bistro table and soaks it in. That's the kind of week it's been—hectic enough to grab some peace like this. Between a jam-packed BOG meeting, and declaring Elsa's tomato business null and void, his days have rolled on—nonstop. There was Jason's boardwalk meeting, too, announcing that he and Maris are back together. Not to mention Cliff's morning workouts with Matt. Then the trailer kitchenette's hot plate conked out, so Cliff had to buy a new one, pronto.

But the week all *started* with his wedding proposal that never happened. And the week *wrapped* with tonight's lackluster Friday night fishing.

So now he's home from fishing and sits in the stillness. The trailer's back door is open to the night. Behind the trailer, there are shingled cottages the next block over. Lamplight from those cottages shines through the trees out back. The moon's rising, too—that massive full moon Kyle was rambling on about earlier.

Still, Cliff just sits there in the quiet.

Until he hears distinct footsteps climbing the four metal stairs out at the front of the trailer. Footsteps—followed by a stern rapping on the steel entry door.

28

"*Now what?*" he asks himself.

As he goes to see who's there, the knocking briefly pauses before starting right up again. When he opens the door, it's to Elsa. She's standing on the top step—*mid-knock*—in her faded jeans, a tank top and light sweater over it all. But it's that rigid, ready-to-knock arm that gets his attention.

"You're making an *awful* lot of racket, Mrs. DeLuca," Cliff says.

"Enough to break a noise ordinance?" Elsa breezes into the trailer, then looks back at him at the still-open door. "You can put the fine on my ... my *ordinance* tab," she says, setting her black straw tote down beside his tanker desk. "Just add it below the fine there for my now-defunct tomato cart business."

"Elsa." Cliff closes the trailer's steel door and turns to her. She's looking around his office space. Her hands alight on his desktop. On a wall shelf. "You *know* I have to enforce ordinances," he insists. "As beach commissioner, it's my job."

"Yes. The rules are the rules. I know. But in life, *sometimes* people make exceptions. Especially for someone they might care about."

"And I do care about you, Elsa."

She only looks over her shoulder at him, then glances at her fingertips. "It's getting dusty in here. When's the last time you cleaned?"

Still standing near the door, Cliff turns up his hands. "Been a while since I've had company."

"I'm sure that's because you've been busy—shutting down charming little businesses. Crisscrossing hazard tape over random tomato carts." As she says it, Elsa's poking around in Cliff's utility closet, then turns to him with a feather duster in her hand. "Don't you think that was an excessive move, Cliff?" She swishes the feathers over his desktop now.

"Excessive? We can't just have pop-up businesses in the community. Ventures starting up at people's whims. Things'll get out of control without jurisdiction." Cliff takes a few steps closer to her as she swipes and sweeps those feathers over his blotter, his computer, his calculator, his multiple pads of sticky notes. "Elsa. You bypassed all Stony Point protocol with that tomato cart."

"But it would've been gone as soon as the tomato crop was gone. A few more days, maybe. A week or two—at most. And you know something? That little cart it ... it made me happy! So you can imagine that now I'm *miffed* at you."

"Well, I had no choice." Cliff walks to his desk and straightens the gavel Elsa just moved in her dusting spree. He restacks the sticky-note pads, too. "If I let one broken rule slip by," he goes on, "petitions will pile up for me to do the same for others."

"Wait." Elsa looks up from the low table she's dusting. Old Stony Point newsletters are splayed there beside a few magazines. "Why aren't you fishing?"

"Fishing?"

"Yes." Dusting promptly resumes as she prattles on. "I went by the rocks to find you, and the guys sent me here. Said you had a chip—or some such thing—on your shoulder tonight. That you were out of sorts." She walks to the trailer's steel door, opens it and goes out to the top step to shake the duster's feathers. For good measure, she taps that duster on the railing there, too, before returning inside. "Seems to me it's been all week," she's saying.

"*What's* been all week?" Cliff asks—as if he doesn't know. As if he doesn't *damn well* know he's been out of sorts—and *why*. It's because of everything from that tanked wedding proposal to a perfectly nice beach bouquet Elsa received—from Mitch Fenwick.

"You've had a *chip* on your shoulder all week, it seems," Elsa's telling him while veering toward the tiny printer room off his trailer office.

"That's because I've had things on my mind."

This stops her dusting. She turns from the printer room's doorway. The feather duster is held aloft. Their eyes cautiously lock.

In that moment's silence, Cliff says nothing. Neither does Elsa, he notices. But she looks like she's about to.

Elsa feels it.

Feels the tension as they silently look only at each other. She feels the words that are begging to burst forth. Words that have nothing to do with tomato carts and more to do with feelings. With confusion. With Mitch, maybe.

That tension is cut by the sudden ringing of Cliff's cell phone.

"Got to take this," Cliff says with a glance at his phone. "It's Nick."

Elsa nods and wanders through the accordion door toward the kitchenette. There, she dusts off the two chairs at the bistro table. And listens to Cliff behind her now.

"Okay. Two things, you say?" he asks into the phone. "Lay the first one on me."

Silence.

Then, "Narrowed *down* the paint colors? What do you mean you can't decide?"

"*Paint colors for what?*" Elsa harshly whispers while popping back into the office.

Cliff waves her off.

"*For here?*" she persists, pointing to the trailer walls.

Cliff turns away from her and barks into the phone. "Can you hold on a sec, Nicholas?" Turning back to Elsa, he puts a hand over his phone. "It's for the *guard* shack."

"*Oooh.* Do you have samples?" she asks.

"No. Well, yes. But Nick has them." Raising his phone again, Cliff also raises an eyebrow at her. "Do you mind now?" he asks Elsa. "Nick's got something else to tell me."

"*Okay, okay.*" Elsa zips her lips before giving Cliff a playful swat with the feather duster as he resumes his call.

"Sorry. I'm still here, Nick. And I'll take a look at those chips again in the morning. But wait, you said there were *two* things to tell me. What else?"

Elsa's moved past the four-panel room divider separating the kitchenette from Cliff's living quarters now. At the end table beside Cliff's futon, she dusts the lamp there, then straightens a throw tossed atop the futon and dusts his framed seascape painting hanging beside it.

"*What?* An accident?" Cliff asks.

Elsa spins around and makes a beeline for the office. "Accident?" she repeats, walking toward Cliff. "Who?"

"*Totaled?*" Cliff shouts into the phone.

"*Who* totaled their car?" Elsa once again swats Cliff with that feather duster. "Someone *here*?"

Cliff covers the phone and whispers, "*It's Maris. But hold on!*"

"Oh my *God!* Maris. Oh my God, oh my God."

"It was a deer?" Cliff holds a hand up toward Elsa as he leans into his phone call with Nick. "Her car swerved before spinning out of control?"

"Is she *okay*?" Elsa jabs Cliff's arm with that feather duster and tries to hear what's being said. "Cliff?"

"Yes." Cliff nods, but holds up an open hand to her while turning back to his call. "Nick, I can't *hear* you. Now say that again."

Silence again, *interminable* silence while Nick explains in Cliff's ear.

Finally, "Uh-huh. Uh-huh. And what about Jason?" Cliff asks into the phone. Then, more eternal silence before he goes on. "All right. I'll stop and see them tomorrow."

"Where? Visit them *where*?" Elsa persists, crowding Cliff now as he sets down his phone. "In the hospital? During visiting hours?"

"No, no." Cliff takes her by the arms and sits her in a straight chair beside his tanker desk. Tugs that feather duster she's clutching and sets that aside, too. "Calm *down*, everything's okay. They're both all right. Maris *and* Jason."

"*Are you certain?*" Elsa whispers, fighting some new knot in her throat.

"Yes. Nick says it was just a close call. Maris' car versus a deer."

With those words—*Maris' car versus a deer*—everything sort of mutes. Cliff goes on with the story. He sits on the edge of his tanker desk and explains how the deer leapt into the street right in front of Maris' car. Jason was following behind in his SUV. They were dropping her car off for service. But Cliff's voice is just a monotone hum as Elsa panics. Her heart races with the thought that she came so close to losing her beloved niece tonight—and never even knew it. While Elsa sat typing emails to Concetta, Maris was grappling with her out-of-control car on some country road. Elsa gives her head a quick shake and focuses on Cliff's words.

"Even the deer is okay," he says. "Eating roadside, happy as can be."

Still, Elsa has to be *sure* Maris isn't hurt. Has to be sure her niece and Jason aren't keeping anything from her—so as not to worry her. So she tells Cliff she needs to hear Maris for herself. Right away.

And he doesn't argue, instead giving a single nod.

"Because I'll *know*, just from her voice," Elsa's saying, all while getting her cell phone from her tote, "if she's fine or not." And she says no more to Cliff—not when Maris promptly answers the call. After Elsa asks how she's doing, Maris reassures her.

"But I'm tired from the whole ordeal," Maris admits.

"*All right, hon.* It's just that, well, I only wanted to hear you. To be *sure* you're fine."

"Oh, Aunt Elsa. You're so sweet. But really, I am. The car's fine, too. *And* Jason."

Elsa presses the phone to her ear. "You're not lying to me? Because I can come over *right* now."

When Maris asks her not to, and says that she's taking it easy, Elsa reluctantly tells her goodnight. "Love you, Maris. Sleep well."

After the call, Elsa turns to Cliff. He's standing at an open trailer window—from where he'd been listening. The night air drifts in; the room is hushed. And what it all does—the whole Maris incident, the near miss with disaster—is make *everything* else seem trivial.

"Maris said to come over tomorrow," Elsa quietly tells Cliff while setting her phone back in her tote. "She's on the couch with the dog now. And is tired, of course."

"What about Jason?"

"Well, apparently Jason drove her home in his SUV after the deer thing, so they'd left her car roadside. He and Kyle are picking it up now."

And that's it. Elsa just sits there in the tin trailer. The feather duster is on Cliff's desk. Only a couple of lights are on, so the trailer is dimly lit. Elsa takes a long breath. Her hands are cupped limply in her lap. All fight is gone from her—the tomato cart fight, her quarrel with Cliff. The only fight that matters tonight is the one that her dear niece just gave to escape a really dire situation.

In the night's silence, Elsa looks over at Cliff—still at the window. She can see he never changed out of his fishing clothes—his lightweight, waterproof fishing jacket that keeps off the sea damp; the short wading boots with special foam cushioning against sharp rocks; his repellent-treated pants protecting against mosquito bites.

Elsa, her voice low, asks him, *"Why do these things keep happening?"* In her pause, then, those *things* run through her mind. Losing her son; mishandlings with the inn and Celia; the shaky Barlow marriage this summer; her own personal missteps. And now, this.

"Come here," Cliff says, opening his arms as he takes a step her way.

Elsa gets up from her seat and walks to him. Just walks straight into those arms. *"Everything's been so hard lately,"* she says, surprising even herself at how tightly she holds onto Cliff.

"It's just life, you know? But everyone's okay, Elsa. That's *all* that matters."

Even after Cliff lightly kisses her moist cheek, she doesn't let go. Leaning in, her head to his shoulder, she closes her eyes and simply breathes a long sigh of relief.

six

"DID YOU CALL THE POLICE?"

Jason glances over at Kyle in the SUV's passenger seat. "I did."

"And reported what happened?"

"Well, there was nothing much to report. Her airbag didn't even deploy." It's dark now as they drive the rural road. There aren't many streetlights on it. Homes are few and far between. Jason's view is mostly of shadowy wooded areas ahead and a midnight-blue sky above—with that massive full moon lighting the way. "I mean, Maris had a close call for sure," he goes on. "But there was no accident. So I just let the authorities know her car is roadside until I can get back to it. This way they won't think someone abandoned it there."

"And why's it going in the shop?" As he asks, Kyle distractedly glances over his shoulder. "Did you say it needed an oil change?"

"And new tires. Maris wants them on before winter."

Kyle twists way around now and looks past the headrest into the backseat. "Hey, man. You have some food in here? What am I smelling?"

"Yeah, that's our dinner. Leftover pizza from Ronni's. It's in the cargo area."

"Knew there was some fine cuisine back there," Kyle says as he resettles in his seat. "And listen, dude, be sure to put good tires on that car of hers."

"I will," Jason says. "Speaking of which …" He nods to the lone vehicle parked half off the road's shoulder up ahead. Pale moonlight falls on the car. "There it is. I'll let you out and you can follow me. You have the keys?"

Kyle gives Maris' key ring a shake as Jason pulls off the road near her car.

Something else happens then, too. Jason has his first laugh of the night. Seriously, it's one he *really* needs. His beautiful wife is all right. Her car is fine. The deer, too. So he has reason to smile, actually. And what does it is watching all six-feet-two of Kyle squeezing into Maris' car a minute later. He slowly climbs in, one leg at a time, and carefully fits himself on the driver's seat.

"*Whoa*," Kyle is saying as his knees practically crunch up to his chest. "Got to push the seat *waaay* back in this one."

⟳

Twenty minutes later, that aroma is more than Kyle can take. All this drama tonight has him working up a hell of an appetite. So when Jason's at the car dealer's drop-off window and pressing his envelope into the key slot, Kyle's lifting a slice of pizza from that take-out box in Jason's SUV. He walks around the side of the vehicle, leans against it and digs into the sauce-and-cheese-covered pizza.

"What's *on* this?" he asks when Jason returns. "It's really good," Kyle adds around a mouthful.

Jason opens the pizza box in the back and grabs a slice, too. "That's chicken and eggplant on it," he says, leaning against the vehicle beside Kyle. "Maris says I need the vegetables."

"You do, guy. So listen to what she says." Standing beneath the parking lot lights, Kyle takes a double bite of the pizza then. "She looks out for you."

Jason nods while chewing his own food. "Damn straight she does. And I thought I was going to lose her tonight."

"That's pretty heavy stuff. Almost crashing her car. Was she going fast? Speeding a little?"

"No. Maybe five, ten miles over the speed limit. But you know, you move at a pretty good clip there on that stretch of road—so fast enough."

"I'll bet she was shaken up."

"Yeah. Me, too." Jason presses the last of his pizza slice into his mouth. "Why do you think I had *you* bring her that tea?" he asks around the food. Holds out his hands, too.

Kyle takes a look. There's no missing the tremor in Jason's fingers. The trembling doesn't stop until Jason shakes it out. "*Shit*," Kyle quietly says.

"Yeah. My heart just about quit beating tonight, man." As Jason walks around to the back of the SUV for another couple of pizza slices, he keeps talking. "Seeing her car fishtail like that … tires squealing. She must've been fighting like mad to get control."

Kyle takes a pizza slice from him. "And there was nothing you could do."

"No. That's the worst of it, you know? Being helpless. Because I knew—I just *knew*—Maris didn't see that second deer," Jason goes on while taking a bite of his pizza slice. "She was still keeping an eye on the first one that crossed. And I couldn't *do* anything except watch my worst nightmare play out."

They're quiet, then, the two of them. Eating, shaking their heads. Whispering a few choice cusses at life's nasty surprises. When Jason talks again, it clues Kyle in, actually, to how close a call Maris faced. There's a lot there, in his friend's voice. In the way it drops. In the way Kyle *barely* hears what he's saying.

"I thought, that's it—I'm going to lose her." Jason lowers the pizza slice he holds. He just stops eating. "*Jesus*," his hoarse voice continues. "After we just got things right again." He blows out a long breath and drops that half-eaten pizza slice back in the box. "I feel so bad for her, Kyle. Handling those few godawful seconds on her own."

"She did it, though. She made it," Kyle says, clapping Jason's shoulder. "I wasn't going to say anything in front of her before—but it's like I told you when we went camping two weeks ago. Remember? When we were driving there, and that deer was grazing on the side of the road? A little too close?"

"I know, man. I know." Jason pulls his keys from his pocket and gets in the SUV.

When Kyle climbs in the passenger side, Jason keeps talking. His voice is serious. "The minute I saw that first deer tonight?" he goes on. "I was already looking for the next one."

⌒⌣

When Jason finally gets home, Maris is on the couch again. She's lying down and watching TV in her pajamas now, back beneath that soft throw. The lights are dim. The TV volume, low. She's quiet, too. Jason notices all this as he leans into the living room doorway with a hello, then puts the last few pizza slices in the fridge. Washes his hands at the kitchen sink. Calls out that her car's all set, that Kyle got it to the dealer—no problem.

Maris is *still* quiet, though, when Jason goes into the living room and sits right beside her on the edge of the couch. Resting a hand on her leg, he leans over and kisses her forehead.

But it's the hand on her leg that feels the shake. A good wave of trembling moves beneath his palm, his fingers. "Hey," he says, rubbing her leg.

"*What's wrong with them?*" Maris asks, quick tears filling her eyes. "It's scaring me, the way they've been doing that."

"Shaking?"

She nods. "But I'm not cold anymore, Jason. So is something wrong with me?"

The shaking in her legs continues. It comes in waves, one after the other. "It'll stop," he assures her.

"But it hasn't all night. The whole time you were gone. I tried to walk it off. Then I'd sit again. And try rubbing them. I put on my pajamas, too."

"It's just adrenaline." Jason, still squeezed in and sitting

41

close beside her on the couch, tucks her hair behind an ear. Softly moves his open hand along her cheek. "It happened to me the day of the bike wreck."

"You were shaking?"

He nods. "I was in and out of consciousness. But I never forgot the shaking. It moved through my whole *body* in waves." The memory comes to him; the feeling, too, of having no physical control over that sensation. It gets him to briefly close his eyes now. The house is quiet. Maris is still, and watching him. He knows it by her touch. By her fingers tracing on his arm. So he shifts on the couch beside her and takes her hand in his. His voice is low and calm when he continues talking. "My doctor explained that during the crash, it's like I was under attack. And my body instantly prepared me for a fight-or-flight response. But that energy had nowhere to go when I just lay there on the pavement, and on the stretcher afterward. Still … my body *had* to expel that energy—and did it by trembling."

Maris takes a quick breath—a gasp, almost. "But I'm *still* shaking, Jason. And so much time's gone by."

"Trust me, Maris. Your body's just taking care of itself right now. *Don't worry*," he whispers, still holding her hand. "I'll sit here with you."

Maris looks down at her legs, then at him. "You don't think I need to go to the hospital, do you? To be sure I'm all right?"

"No, sweetheart. All I need you to do is take a long, *slow* breath. Okay?"

She hesitates, then does it—deeply filling her lungs.

"And another." When Maris breathes again, he goes on. "Now get comfy and close your eyes."

She starts to resist, but gives in when he merely squints at her.

And when her eyes are closed, Jason rubs her legs as she lies there. He shifts further down the couch, and his hand moves along her thighs, her calves. *Gentle, gentle.* His every touch in the quiet house calms her. The TV, meanwhile, flickers in the shadowy room. And the dog lies nearby on the floor.

The whole time, Jason says only a few concerned words. Asks if she's feeling better. Tells her she's doing fine. He eventually gets up just to crack a window and let in some of the night's salt air. Its tonic might help her. When he returns to the couch, he sits on the far end and sets Maris' legs across his lap.

Adjusts the knitted throw atop her legs.

Massages her calves.

Whispers that he's so glad, so very glad, she's here with him.

seven

AFTER MARIS FALLS ASLEEP UPSTAIRS later, Jason sits on his bedside chair. He doesn't shut off the dim lamp on the nightstand. Doesn't take off his prosthetic leg. Doesn't really move—other than to lean forward, elbows on his knees—and drop his head. Sitting there like that, he hears Maris' soft breathing. It's regular. She's truly resting now.

But he can't.

He never let on how shook up the night got him. Didn't let on to Maris. Not much to Kyle, either. *Damn.* Jason finally sits back, blows out a breath and rubs the back of his neck. It's been kinked up all night. After giving Maris one last look, he reaches over to lightly touch her shoulder, murmurs *Love you*, then shuts off the lamp and heads downstairs. That trembling that Maris felt all evening? Jason feels some, too. Like he has to keep giving his arms a shake. Roll his shoulders. Work off the night's anxiety. So he paces a little. Turns off the TV. Grabs a drink of water.

Outside, that big full moon casts its pale light on the earth.

Might as well drop some on him, too. He gives the dog a low whistle as he heads down the hallway to the front foyer. Behind him, Maddy scrambles out of her bed. Her nails click on the hardwood floor.

"*Shh*, Maddy," Jason says as he lifts his sweatshirt and the house key from the table there. "Come on," he says, opening the front door. "Let's go work out the kinks."

~

Kinks. Thoughts. Fears. Whatever.

Beneath the moonlight, it all comes out. The beach is deserted at this hour. In the glow of the heavy moon, there's no missing that. So Jason feels safe here. It's just himself, his dog and the sea. As he walks, he stretches his arms. Rolls his neck. All the while, gentle waves lap onshore.

"*She made it, Neil*," he eventually whispers while looking out over the water. "I've never been so afraid. And so relieved."

You're a lucky man, Jason hears back as those waves break in a silver froth on the sand, hissing over and over.

"I am. But came really close to saying something else tonight." Jason drags a hand through his hair. "To saying what a lucky man I'd *been*." He takes a deep breath of the night's damp salt air. "To have *had* Maris in my life." Even uttering those words to his brother, or his spirit, or just the lonely sea out there? It chokes Jason up. Because he knows. He knows that even *Maris* doesn't realize how close she came to dying in that car.

But Jason does know.

He was behind her vehicle, after all. He saw the swerve. The fishtailing. Saw the looming maple and oak trees just off the road. They're the type of trees one might see a withered bouquet of flowers laid beneath. Or a rudimentary crucifix propped against. If Maris hit her brakes just so much harder, the skid might've been that much stronger. Strong enough to *not* recover control. To send the car into the solid tons of a towering oak tree.

"I could've been saying what a beautiful woman Maris *was*. And how she blessed my life by briefly being in it," Jason quietly goes on as he walks the hard-packed sand. A slight sea breeze skims off the night water. It grazes his whiskered face. Lifts his hair. "That in her wedding vow, she promised to be with me always. And she *will* be, in here." Jason pats his heart—but only for a second. Because his hand moves to his eyes then, swiping at some sudden tears there. If he feels that emotion from Maris only *brushing* with disaster—and surviving—anything else would've crushed him.

Crushed him.

"*Jesus Christ, Neil,*" Jason nearly whispers as he reaches the rocky ledge at the end of the beach. Beyond, a dark shadow of woods frames the line of boulders. "What a difference a second or two makes in life. One lousy *second.*"

The sea breeze gets small waves splashing on the rocks. *You know that more than anyone*, Jason hears as he feels that breeze on his skin.

"I do … I do," Jason says into the night. He turns then, whistling for Maddy to follow him back down the beach. "That second or two was on Maris' side tonight."

Wasn't on ours when we needed it, bro, he hears—right as

Maddy runs past, her dog collar jangling.

"Nope." Walking along the tideline, Jason scoops up a few sea pebbles. "Was a bleak day we had then." He skims a stone out over the water, and in the moonlight that skipping stone sends a silver spray skyward. "Today could've been just as bleak." He shakes his head and keeps walking, crossing the beach now and heading to the footpath. "My life would've been over tonight, too—without Maris."

But it's not, Neil's voice barely comes to him. Or the dune grasses whisper. Jason turns his head, straining to listen.

Nothing. There are no more words. Only Jason's thoughts.

Or one thought.

Damn, he had to be reminded *again* today—though he's always known it. Life *can* go either way. From one second to the next.

He looks up at that moonlit sky now and gives a slight salute, all with immense gratitude that he isn't talking to two spirits tonight.

eight

STILL, JASON COULDN'T SLEEP.

Not well, anyway. The mere possibility of his life upending again had him toss and turn much of the night. Had him reach out in the darkness and lightly touch Maris' long brown hair. Had him turn to the window where moonlight spilled in and blow out a cautious breath. Had him turn back and slip an arm around Maris, pulling her close to him in the night.

By sunup Saturday, he knows, though.

Better to get out of bed than to wake Maris with his fretting. It's important that she rest. So he's up and at 'em early. After feeding Maddy, he takes a quick shower followed by coffee on the deck. And the next thing he knows, he's channeling his anxiety into yard work. Hell, he'd been gone for three weeks, home for one. Now the neglected high grass and shaggy shrubs don't escape his scrutiny.

"Okay," Jason figures as he downs the last of his coffee. "Time to fix up the Barlow property."

So with the dog tagging along, he swaps his sneakers for serious work boots. Next? Pull the shed keys from his cargo shorts pocket and get to it. One piece at a time, he arranges his yard equipment on the lawn outside the shed. Hedge trimmer. Telescoping loppers. Lawn edger, for the driveway later. Leaf blower. Rake. Aluminum stepladder. He's got enough projects lined up to keep busy all day so that Maris can just take it easy inside.

First up? Trim the overgrown hedges in the side yard. So he hauls the ladder there and sets it up at those hedges, careful of Maddy lying in the shade. He gets the loppers next. Puts on his work gloves, carefully climbs the ladder and begins. He starts by cutting off dead branches and some of the old growth. Slowly he moves along the hedges, resetting the ladder as necessary. But the sun's rising higher now, leaving Jason squinting against the glare. So he sets down his loppers, locks Maddy on the deck and goes in the house for a baseball cap. There's a small pile of them on his closet shelf. He'll slip in and grab one.

⁓

Halfway up the stairs, there's a noise. It has Jason freeze. And tip his head. But he can't place the sound. So he takes slow steps until he gets to the upstairs landing. Quietly then, he walks down the hall before stopping—right outside their bedroom. There, he drops his head and listens again.

Shit.

49

It's Maris; he knows it.

It's Maris sobbing.

So he turns into the doorway and the sight stops him. Wearing her blue nightshirt, she's sitting up in bed—but her hands cup her face as she gives heaving, heaving sobs. The sound is guttural and desperate. Her shoulders shake. Her whole body is bent into those cupped hands. Each sob just wrenches her body. It's obvious, too, that she's trying to keep those sobs quiet, trying to quell them, the way she's pressing her face, her eyes, deep into those cupped hands.

"*Hey, hey*. What's the matter?" Jason asks, hurrying to the bed now. "You're all right," he tells her as he sits on the edge of the mattress. "Everything's good."

"*Jason*," Maris barely manages as he brushes back her tear-soaked hair, touches her wet face, drenched eyelashes. "I thought you were outside," she says between shuddering sobs.

"I was. But I needed a hat." He presses aside her hair again. "What's *wrong?*" he asks while cradling her face.

Maris places a hand over his. Gives him a sad smile, too. "*It's just last night*," she whispers before the tears come again. "*And what almost happened. When I think of it …*"

She doesn't say more. It's obvious she can't. The sobs rise again, such that he just takes all of her in his arms right there and holds her. And lets the cries come. Lets the sadness and fear wash out of her. The whole time, he strokes her hair, her back.

"*Shh, shh*," he says, rocking a little with her still in his arms. Her body feels fragile and small, like this crying is *so* much bigger than she is somehow.

Still she doesn't talk. Instead there are gasps for air between her sobs.

"*Hey*," Jason gently says, pulling away. "This is about more than last night."

She nods, then swipes at her tears. "It is. It's everything, Jason. It's about what we almost lost, you and me, these past few weeks. Each other."

"But we're okay, sweetheart. We made it through."

Now? Now she shakes her head. "No. Because it's about you, too."

"Me?"

Another nod. "You're always right there when I need you." A gasp, then, "Like last night. And ... and I *wasn't* there for you this summer—when you really needed me."

"Oh, Maris. It's not like that." He tips up her wet chin. "It's just not like that."

"No?" She takes a shuddering breath. "I got to run to you last night. But who'd you get to run to this summer? Your brother gone ten years, the anniversary of that accident stirring up all sorts of things, and ... and," she goes on, slapping her hand on the mattress, "I turned my *back* on you?"

Jason just looks long at her. At her damp, brown eyes. At the pain of a lot of mistakes and missteps this summer. At so much more than her swerving her car last night.

And he pulls her close and holds her again. She presses her face into his shoulder and he runs his hand down her hair. Doesn't let go of his beautiful Maris, not until she calms.

~

Minutes later, Maris is alone in the room. As suddenly as Jason had come in, he left her there. But he also told her to stay put; he'd be right back.

And she did stay put—after a quick trip to the bathroom. There, she splashed cold water on her face. Handful after handful, trying to wash away her tears. Her thoughts. She brushed her hair, too, before going back to the bedroom and sitting on the bed.

Waiting. And pressing wrinkles out of the sheets. And waiting more.

Finally, Jason's footsteps come up the stairs. She hears him talking to Maddy, who must be right behind him. The dog's tuned in to every emotion of the house.

When Jason turns into the bedroom, he's carrying a box that he sets on his bedside chair before sitting with her on the unmade bed again.

"Jason." Maris takes a clear breath now. "I'm so embarrassed about before. Crying like that."

"Don't be. It was a release for you. An emotional release. You can't keep all those feelings bottled up inside." He takes her hand in his. "I *had* a release at Ted's. Talked to a lot of people there. Ted, Eva. Shane. Celia and Elsa. Kyle, even."

"I didn't talk a lot while you were gone. Not much to my sister. Or Elsa. It all felt too private."

Jason nods while stroking her hand. "There's more, Maris."

"What is it?"

"I had a panic attack on the beach a few weeks ago. At Sea Spray."

"*Oh, Jason.*"

"I did. It was the night before Neil's Memorial Mass—and I couldn't breathe. The more I tried, the more my lungs closed up. I was actually afraid I'd pass out, so I just sat on the sand that night. Sat there and tried to drag in a breath—which I couldn't. Even Maddy got all riled up, nudging me. Whining. But it wouldn't stop, Maris, the way everything started spinning. And I was sweating. The poor dog finally just lay beside me. And I didn't know if I'd make it until I started up with the tactical breathing my father taught me and my brother. From when Dad was in the jungles in 'Nam."

"Counting out your breaths."

Jason nods. "It worked, but took time that night. And effort. And sometimes? Sometimes it felt like Neil was right there, helping me. *Whispering the count.*" Jason takes a long breath now. "Eventually I calmed down. Got a good, deep breath. Then another. So I came out of it. But that panic attack was *my* release, like you had today. You never had any outlet while we were separated, until now."

Sitting there on the bed, Maris squeezes his hand. "So what'd you bring up?"

Jason reaches for the box. He lifts out his father's pewter hourglass.

"Jason, I use this writing."

"I know. But we can use it for this, too."

"For what?"

He lifts an architectural journal and pen from the box now, draws a few lines on some pages, labels the columns. "We're going to start a tally of the lost hours we have to recover."

"What are you talking about?"

"Remember our dinner at Bella's, when I first came

back home? And we talked about losing three weeks of time together?"

"Well, sure. But—"

"I did some calculating," Jason explains, turning the lined pad to her. "This summer, we were apart for three weeks. That's twenty-four hours a day, times seven days a week, times three weeks. Which equals 504 lost hours. Multiply that by sixty minutes, and we racked up 30,240 minutes apart. Or thereabouts."

"Jason!" Maris smiles and looks up at him. "We'll never get all that back."

"Why not? So far we've logged twenty minutes."

"Twenty minutes?"

"Yep. Twenty steamy minutes when you set my alarm clock early the other day. *You* told *me* you were getting back our lost time. So," he says, pointing to his graphed-and-outlined page, "I've noted those twenty minutes and deducted them from the total. We now are working on recouping 30,220 lost minutes."

She gives a slight laugh, then. "Okay. Okay, so what do you have in mind with this tally?" Maris holds up his architectural-pad-turned-lost-time log. "What are you suggesting?"

Jason looks long at her. Tucks back a strand of her hair, too. "To start? I'm suggesting that we stay in bed today. All day. Both of us."

"*What?* What about the hedges?"

"I'll do them tomorrow. But we'll grab a day together, today."

"Oh come on, Jason." Maris fluffs her pillow against the headboard and sits back in bed. "We can't stay here in bed all day. And do what?"

54

Jason shrugs. "Not much. Read the paper." He takes the morning's edition of *The Day* out of the box. "Doze." He lifts a sleep mask from the box. "Feel the salt air drift into the room." He gets up and opens a window, then sits on the messy bed again. "Play cards. Or, or you can read me some of your *Driftline* passages."

"*Hmm*. I can paint my nails?" Maris asks.

"Anything."

"Give you a kiss or two? Have a coffee in bed?"

"That's right." Jason kisses the top of her head. "You know, easy. Easy. Just catch our breath."

Maris suddenly hops out of bed and looks her own tired nightshirt up and down. "But really. I need to shower first."

"That's fine." Jason gets up, too. He walks to her and touches her splotchy face before turning to their bed. "But dress comfortably afterward," he says over his shoulder. "We don't have to go *anywhere*," he tells her, already getting her pillow fluffed for the day.

～～

Once Maris is in the shower, Jason begins their catch-up and slow-down day. First he fixes up the entire bed. He gets the wrinkles out of the sheets. Tucks and folds them just so. Folds down their coverlet, too. Then he opens all the window shades, and the windows, too. It's a warm day, and the September air feels good. He turns, then, and takes in the sight of the room. A little freshening up is in order, so he straightens Maris' dresser top. Drops some earrings and a necklace into her jewelry box. Refolds a tee she'd tossed there. On her nightstand, he puts a brass ship-wheel paperweight on some manuscript papers she'd been working on. He gets their new crank-up radio out of his box and puts it on his dresser.

Then he steps back. Sunlight streams in the windows. Birdsong makes its way into the room, too. Some random robin sings a happy tune in the big maple tree in the yard. The bed is casually neatened. The newspaper, and pens, and magazines are stacked bedside.

And Jason runs a hand along his scarred jaw as he admires the tidied-up room. Because he knows. Maris' distress earlier wasn't from just the near collision last night. It's from their nearly broken marriage.

From their *fully* missed two-year wedding anniversary.

From 504 *hours* of missed moments and laughs and talks and touches.

So yes, he thinks when he turns and goes downstairs. They'll log every lost hour recovered and each missed minute reclaimed ... and *some* day? They'll catch up.

⁓

Maris bends over in her robe and towel-dries her hair. The bathroom is steamy from the shower; the upstairs is quiet. Still drying her hair, she straightens and wanders back to the bedroom. Jason's not there. Neither is Maddy. So she tiptoes to the stairs and descends them. Softly, softly, her bare feet pad along the cool hardwood floor toward the kitchen. When she gets close, she presses against the hallway wall, all while patting that bath towel on her wet hair. Inch by inch, she scoots closer to the kitchen until she can peek in.

The first thing she notices is Maddy lying on the deck outside the slider.

Second? Jason, still in his yard-work shorts, tee and boots. He's standing at the stove and coating a baking dish with nonstick cooking spray. Something's sizzling on a skillet on the burner. Butter, maybe. There's a large plate beside the stove that's covered with sliced apple wedges. He picks them up now and adds each wedge to the skillet. And oh, the aroma filling that room! It's *divine*. As those apples sizzle, Jason gets a carton of half-and-half from the fridge. And eggs. And a loaf of cinnamon bread from the bread drawer.

And looks a little lost.

He keeps glancing at whatever recipe he's preparing, then checks the stovetop. And his ingredients. And runs his thumb along his scarred jaw. And wipes his palms on his shorts before finding the vanilla extract in a cabinet.

And Maris sees. It's all over his face. In his tired eyes. In the shadows beneath them.

He's worried.

He's *so* worried.

And he wants to make breakfast and make *everything* better. Wants every logged hour to count.

So Maris silently turns away, hurries upstairs and blow-dries her hair. That done, she quickly slips into her olive jogger loungewear: cuffed, loose pants and slouchy, short-sleeve top.

Just seeing Jason *trying* like that, well, it's enough to bring sweet tears—the good kind—to her eyes.

nine

ON THE WAY TO CELIA'S cedar-shingled guest cottage behind the inn, something gets Elsa to look twice. It's the cottage's diamond-shaped stained-glass window reflecting rays of early morning sunlight. The blues and reds and golds softly shimmer this September Saturday.

But Elsa keeps walking. She has little time to spare before her hair appointment. And she wants to catch Celia before the day unfolds. So Elsa heads straight up the steps to Celia's front porch. Two wicker rocking chairs sit side by side behind the pretty railing. Maybe they can talk right there; it's such a cozy spot. Surely sitting on those rockers, Celia will accept her apology for mishandling the inn's grand opening. It'll just take a few minutes. Then they might have lunch together later. Talk more. Work on getting their friendship back.

Feeling optimistic, Elsa stops at the wood-framed screen door and looks inside. Sunlight glows on the white board-and-batten walls. Fluffed pillows line the sofa. Celia's guitar case leans against an end table. Elsa gives a friendly knock on the door while calling through the screen. "*Yoo-hoo!* Celia?"

Moments later, Celia's approaching from the other side of the screen door. Her hair is in a loose side braid; she's dressed in a tee and faded cuffed shorts. She's also maneuvering the last of a piece of toast into her mouth while holding Aria in her arms.

"Elsa," Celia says, stopping at the screen and rubbing her crumb-covered fingers together. "Good morning." She shifts Aria then and waves the baby's tiny hand in Elsa's direction.

"Hello, little love," Elsa says, touching the screen before looking back at Celia. "Am I interrupting your breakfast, Cee?"

"That's okay. It's a working breakfast." Celia bends and kisses Aria's head when the baby keeps cooing to Elsa. "I'm writing lesson plans with my coffee."

"Oh, good! Good! It's important to be prepared. When do your classes start?"

"Few more weeks still. Which is why I can't invite you in, unfortunately. Right after I eat, I'm making a zip trip to Addison. There's a shed behind my father's house, where I keep the décor for my home staging. I need some pieces for my class."

"I see." Elsa backs up a step. "Maybe I'll see you when you get back?"

"Of course." Celia gives a small smile. "Was it something important?"

Elsa looks at her for a long second. "It can wait."

"All right. We'll catch up then?"

"Sure. That's fine." Elsa blows a kiss to Aria through the screen, then turns to leave. "Oh, one more thing!" she calls, turning back from the bottom step. "Celia!"

Celia and the baby reappear at the screen door. "What's up?"

"Did you hear about Maris?" Elsa asks.

"Maris?" Cautiously, Celia opens the screen door and steps barefoot onto the porch. "I didn't. Is she okay?"

"Well. She *says* she is." Elsa squints in the vague direction of the Barlow house, then turns back to Celia and tells her about Maris' near-accident, and the sudden deer, and the skidding car. "We all had quite a scare. Maris, included."

Celia hoists Aria in her arms to better see her watch. "*Hmm*. We'll be back from my dad's after lunch." She looks to Elsa then. "Maybe I'll go see Maris this afternoon. Just to say hi and, you know, check in."

Elsa nods. "Me, too. I have a few things to do this morning, though, including a stop at the salon in a little bit. So ... hair appointment first. Maris, later."

⌒⌣

As if.

As if whenever Elsa least expects it, a certain someone doesn't go and show up in her life.

Show up with a reminder for a farm breakfast, maybe.

Or with a charming garden cart in tow, wheeled over from his cottage-on-the-beach.

Or with a discreet flower arrangement left at her doorstep.

60

Or he shows up roadside to rescue her from a potential *tap-and-go* traffic violation.

Or shows up when she steps out her door—like right now—as she's on her way to that hair appointment.

Because, oh that gray vehicle parking in front of the inn is *very* familiar. That ... that *safari*-style vehicle with the roof off. With the grab handles to hold onto when speeding along, the warm summer wind whipping by.

With the very familiar *driver* stepping out—right now—too.

"Elsa!" Mitch Fenwick calls as he stops there and waves her over.

Well. Elsa looks this way, then that. For what, she's not sure. Maybe it's just to buy time to fix a wayward wisp of hair. And to lift her cat-eye sunglasses to the top of her head. And subtly straighten her ruffled cap-sleeve white blouse over her cropped navy-and-white striped pants. Or, hell. Maybe it's to check for *absolute* certain that she won't be caught dallying here with this guy.

"Mitch," she says when she finally steps toward him. Her leather slide sandals skim the grass as she crosses the inn's front yard.

"I have some bags of groceries to unload," he explains, motioning to the stuffed food bags in the backseat of his vehicle. "Was hoping to briefly catch you before anything spoils."

"To *catch* me?" Elsa asks. *Shoot, it must be about those doorstep flowers!* she suddenly thinks. The midweek bouquet of wild roses and mini sunflowers and beach grasses that Mitch left on her stoop Wednesday—and that *Cliff* discovered.

61

And that she never acknowledged in her busy days since.

"Oh, Mitch. The flowers. They are beautiful," she's saying as she crosses the lawn toward where he's standing. He's got on a tan utility shirt and casual black pants. The shirt is loose at the collar, showing a leather choker around his neck. There's a canvas-brimmed hat on his head, too.

A hat he's tipping to her as she nears. "Flowers?" he asks.

Elsa nods. "Carol's latest creation. The flowers you left on my stoop?"

"Of *course*. With those wild grasses Carol added, I *did* think of your magical winding beach path."

"And what a sweet surprise in my day that bouquet was." Elsa smiles as she nears him. "Thank you for that!"

"My pleasure, Elsa," Mitch says while sweeping off his hat and giving a small bow. "I'm *so* glad you like them. But … it's actually another surprise I'm here about."

"Really?"

Mitch nods and settles his hat on his head again. "I was even *more* surprised to see that tomato cart of yours returned to beneath my cottage stilts."

"Oh, that." Elsa stops at the curb and pulls her car keys from her purse. "Jason dropped the cart off there yesterday morning."

"I must've missed him. Had classes to teach at the college." Mitch reaches out and gives Elsa's hand a squeeze. "But I wanted to check that everything was *okay*. I know you enjoyed that side hustle you had going on. And surely your tomato plants are thriving in this late-summer heat?"

"They are!" Elsa glances toward the blazing sun in the sky, then at her watch ticking away the minutes to her hair appointment. "But apparently my tomato cart was in direct violation of a Stony Point ordinance and was promptly shut down by the Board of Governors."

"Shut down? That quaint little vegetable stand? Now that seems mighty heartless to me."

"Yes, well. It's all over now, my ... side hustle. But I'd like to thank you, Mitch—and Carol, too—for the use of the cart." Elsa steps backward toward her car in the driveway. "For a few days, it brought a lot of happiness."

"But what about all those tomatoes growing in your Sea Garden?"

"With my cart gone, I've been busy canning them." Keys in hand, Elsa turns more toward her car. "Which gives me an idea," she calls over her shoulder. "Can I drop a few jars at your place? As a gesture of gratitude for use of the cart."

"Why sure." Mitch draws a hand down his goatee and squints at Elsa. "It's about time I learned to make pasta sauce anyway."

"What?" Elsa turns completely around and eyes him. "You've *never* made tomato sauce? I mean," she goes on, walking in his direction again. "You? *Bon vivant* of that Coca-Cola cake? And *connoisseur* of a certain sunrise banana pudding?"

Mitch only shrugs. Well, he shrugs with a distinct *twinkle* in his eye. Crosses his arms over his chest, too, while leaning on his safari-style vehicle.

"So all those specialties, but ... no sauce?" Elsa asks.

"Not any recipe I'm proud of. Matter of fact, got some store-bought jars in the bags behind me."

Elsa simply shakes her head with a sad *tsk-tsk*. But she's

smiling, too, all while not taking her sights off Mitch's still-twinkling eyes. Not until she remembers that darn hair appointment and twists her watch around to see the time. "*Okay*. How about if I drop off those canned tomatoes?" she asks, turning to her car again and actually getting the door open this time. Then? Then she stops and turns back. "I'll get you started on a pot of sauce at the same time," she calls to Mitch.

"Now I'd *like* that. This Tuesday sound okay? After my class gets out? I reckon construction oughta be wrapped for the day then."

"Tuesday?" Elsa gets inside her car now. Closes the door and rolls down the window, too. Starts the engine and calls out before putting the car in gear, "Tuesday's good. Text me a time, Mitch? Because I really have to go now," she says, putting the car in reverse and slowly backing out of the driveway. "Late for an appointment!" she adds when he gives a friendly thumbs-up and a wave.

～

Twenty minutes later, in the nick of time, Elsa lands in the salon chair with a long sigh. Her stylist flips open a black cape and settles it around her shoulders, then touches her hair as they face the mirror.

"The usual, Elsa?" her stylist asks her reflection. "Freshen your honey highlights?" she adds, lifting a few strands of hair.

Elsa nods. "A trim, too. Especially my layers. They've really grown out some."

Minutes later, her stylist begins painting on honey-colored dye and clipping on sheets of silver foil. "Okay, now. So ... tell me what's new, Elsa," she says, lifting and dabbing a wide strand of hair before slipping that foil beneath the painted wisp. "Anything exciting?"

"Oh, what's new? *Ha!*" Elsa looks at her watch and settles in the salon chair. Leans back with a deep breath. "Hold on to your mixing bowl," she tells the stylist's reflection in the mirror right as she's painting and foiling a face-framing strand. "Because we have a couple of hours here. That should be enough time for me to catch you up."

ten

SO FAR, SO GOOD, MARIS thinks of Jason's plan later Saturday morning.

It's quiet in their bedroom as it all begins—as grains of sand silently fall in the pewter hourglass and they recover some of their lost time together. A scant sea breeze drifts in the open windows and stirs the sheer curtains. Occasionally, there's a cry of a seagull swooping out over the bluff. And Maddy's gnawing on her rope-bone over in front of Maris' dresser.

But that's it for sounds.

Well, that and the clicking of forks on dishes. And some satisfied *Mmms*. She and Jason are too busy wolfing down the syrup-drizzled baked apple French toast Jason made to say much of anything else. Every now and then an *Oh my God* is whispered. *So good*. But little else. They just work on that baked cinnamon bread covered with gooey apple slices and slightly caramelized maple syrup.

"I can *so* get used to this," Maris finally lets on around a mouthful. Leaning against pillows propped against the headboard, she adjusts the breakfast tray on her lap. "Sitting in bed having homemade French toast?"

Jason nods beside her. "Me, too," is all he manages while lifting a heaping forkful of the food to his mouth. He sets the fork down then, and picks up a pencil and journal.

"What are you doing?" Maris asks him.

He turns the journal and shows the rough drawing of their bedroom. "Sketching our morning."

"Would you look at that." Maris takes the journal. "There's our windows facing the bluff," she says, her finger tracing the drawing. "And the end of our bed, here." She looks more. There's part of his old wooden bureau—complete with valet and change dish on top. "Your dresser, too," she muses, looking up at the actual dresser then back at his sketch. "So … this is kind of our view from bed?"

"It is." Jason takes the journal from her and drags his pencil back and forth, back and forth, shading in the dog on the floor. "Thought I'd put it in our lost-time log. Keeping a visual record of some of the days we recover."

Maris spears a strawberry half on her plate and drags it through some syrup. "That's really nice," she distractedly says.

"Trying to make a dent in those three weeks' worth of missing hours," Jason goes on, still sketching in details. He looks up from the page to an open window, then back to the page.

Mid-food-picking, Maris glances over at him on the bed. He's still dressed to do yard work—but has taken off his work boots—so is really casual in his cargo shorts and some old Yale tee. That baseball cap he needed earlier is flung over the bedpost. "Well, be sure to minus an hour for our breakfast in bed," she reminds him while chewing and watching him sketch.

"I will." He sets his dish on the nightstand. "Going to read the newspaper first," he says, reaching for it beside him. He sips from his coffee cup, then snaps the paper open on his breakfast tray. "Want a section?"

"The arts."

"All right. Arts for you. Front page for me."

Maris drops the arts section on the mattress. No way can she start reading before dabbing, swiping and lifting every last delicious morsel of food off her plate. Every bit of soft, golden baked apple wedges topping her cinnamon-swirled French toast lightly browned at the crusts. Her fork slices through the syrup-laced bread, the drizzled apple pieces. Her eyes flutter closed with the flavors.

There's another noise she notices then ... with her eyes closed in the bedroom touched by a salt-air breeze. It's the soft rustle of newspaper as Jason turns the pages beside her.

⌒

"I'm at the Barlows'," Kyle says into the phone. He's on Jason's front porch, but sits on the stoop while talking to Lauren. "Stopping in on my way to the diner. Just to be sure they're *really* okay. Couldn't legit tell for certain last night. They were that shot."

"Well, let Maris know I'll drop by later?" Lauren asks. "Maybe I'll bring her something. Something to cheer her up."

"Yeah. Yeah, that'd be nice." As he talks, Kyle notices Jason's hedge trimmers and a ladder over at the bushes along the side yard.

"I'll come after lunch," Lauren is saying. "It's so warm today, I'm taking the kids for a beach morning first."

Kyle stands then and slightly stretches. "Grab it while you can. It's mid-September already."

And a flawless September, too. Warm and easy—custom-made for chillin'. When he hangs up with Lauren, he straightens his black work tee and black pants, then gives a good knock at the door.

And waits. "*Come on, come on,*" he whispers, about to knock again.

But before he has a chance to, Jason stops him from an upstairs window. "That you, Bradford?" he calls out.

Kyle steps off the porch for a look at the paned windows above it. Jason's in the front guest bedroom. He opened the screen and is partially leaning outside to talk to Kyle—whose truck is parked at the curb.

"Yo, *bro*," Kyle yells, shielding his eyes as he looks to that second-floor window. "Yeah, it's me."

"Door's unlocked. Come on up," Jason tells him, motioning to Kyle. "Grab a coffee in the kitchen on the way."

Before Kyle can say more, Jason's backed out of the window and closed the screen. So Kyle opens the front door to Maddy waiting there. "Hey, girl," he says, brusquely rubbing the dog's head before walking down the hallway to the kitchen. There, he can't help it. He lets out a low whistle at the reno Maris orchestrated. He saw it last night, but has a better look now. "*Top shelf,*" he whispers, taking in the island's silvery-gray quartz, the denim-blue base, the stonework around the stove. Everything. The stainless-steel state-of-the-art appliances. The two crystal pendant chandeliers. Maddy settles in a sunny spot at the open slider then. "You've got the right idea," he tells her while pouring his coffee. Then he heads back down the dark paneled hallway and up the old wooden stairs.

But Kyle also *considerably* slows his step on the way up. Slows his step and tips his head to better hear the Barlows' conversation in the bedroom. Once he reaches the landing, he actually stops to be sure of their talk coming from behind a partially closed door.

From Maris: "*Now*, Jason. Stop it *now.*" Some quiet, then, "*No!* You went too far!"
And from Jason: "Here? Feel good there?"
Maris' dejected reply: "No, I don't feel *anything*. Try again."
An exasperated Jason then: "*Again?* We've done this how many times already?"

"*Whoa*," Kyle interrupts from the hallway, then lightly pushes open their bedroom door—and quickly covers his eyes. "You guys decent?"
"Come on in, yeah," Jason says.
Kyle doesn't know if he dares, but what the hell. He turns into the room to see Jason finagling an oscillating pedestal fan. "*Seriously*, dude? *That's* what's going on? You've got an a/c in the window, you know."
"Eh. It's half busted." As he says it, Jason's still adjusting that fan.

"And too noisy," Maris says from where she's lounging on the bed. "So Jason's trying to aim the fan at us."

Kyle sets his coffee on a dresser top. "*I've* got this," he tells them, giving Jason a shove. "Hell, wasn't sure *what* I was walking in on here," he adds while shifting the fan to the left some.

"Kyle!" Maris scolds from the bed, where she's getting every last bit of some breakfast food off a plate. "*Really?*"

He shrugs and turns on the fan. "Just saying, from my end … well, if you could've heard yourselves."

"*Stop*, Kyle!" Maris insists.

"Maris." Jason, sitting on the bed now, nudges her. "He didn't *mean* anything by it. Just, you know, maybe thought we were messing around."

"*No*. I know *that*! I meant stop the *fan*! He had it aimed perfectly—*right* on us." She sets her dish on the nightstand and resettles herself sitting against the headboard. "Now we have to wait for it to come around again."

"Okay. So pay attention, guys," Kyle says, watching the fan oscillate.

"Make sure it's set on low," Maris instructs. "We just want a *little* breeze."

"Fine. Got it." Kyle adjusts the controls. "Get ready now. Here it comes."

And after two more full oscillations, two rounds of *No, you just missed!* and a disappointing *Almost*, and Jason telling him to *Focus*, Kyle nails it.

Stops the oscillating fan right *on* them, grabs his coffee off the dresser and takes a seat on Jason's bedside chair. "*Ah*. Nice having a chair in the bedroom like this," he says, leaning back and sipping his hot coffee.

"That's my leg chair," Jason explains from the bed, where he appears to be doing some crossword puzzle in the newspaper. "I'm in that seat at the end of every day," he says while penciling in some word. "Take off my leg there."

"*All right*. The king's throne." Kyle looks at Maris then. "And how're *you* feeling, after that ordeal last night?"

"Better, Kyle," she tells him. "I'm just taking it easy today."

"Really surprised to meet you guys up *here*, though," Kyle remarks, taking in the spread-out newspaper sections on the bed. The dirty breakfast dishes on the nightstands. Empty coffee cups. "Thought you'd maybe be out on the deck on a sweet morning like this."

"This was Jason's idea." Maris reaches over and runs her fingers over his scruffy jaw. "He said we should while away the hours in bed. Kick back a little."

"You and Lauren oughta try it," Jason tells Kyle, hitching his head at him. "Staying in bed all day."

"Yeah. Tell me that after you have two kids to take care of. Support. Raise." Kyle gets up and walks to one of the opened windows. "Plus I don't have your bluff view." Looking out on the vista of blue water and blue skies, he takes a long breath of the tangy salt air.

"Hm. Stuck on this one," Jason muses while pointing to a blank word on the crossword puzzle.

Sitting cross-legged beside him on the bed, Maris leans over. "Give me a clue for a down word near it. We can start to fill it *that* way."

"Hey guys, try this. Works like a charm," Kyle says, turning from the window now. "First find *all* the clues that need a plural word and put in the s. You'll be surprised how many blanks you fill in that way." As he says it, he's picking up dirty dishes and cups from the two nightstands, plus his own emptied coffee cup. Grabs soiled napkins and silverware next, carefully stacks it all and heads to the door. "I got to get to the diner, but am super glad you're both okay," he tells them over his shoulder. "I'll load up your dishwasher on my way out," he calls from the upstairs landing.

"Thanks, guy!" Jason yells as Kyle goes down the stairs.

"You got it, Barlows," Kyle yells back.

And he knows. Balancing that tower of dirty dishes, Kyle walks to the kitchen and knows. *Anyone* could just tell. From the dishwasher, he glances up at the ceiling in the vague direction of the Barlow bedroom. Those two are *ensconced* in that little den of comfort and love for hours and hours to come. *No* one's getting them out of there today— no way, no how.

"*Yep, they'll be all right*," Kyle says to himself when he finally walks out the front door.

⌐⌐⌐

Quiet again.

So Jason finishes that crossword puzzle. In the next half hour, he gets every word filled in. Grabs fresh coffee downstairs for himself and Maris afterward. Settles once more on the bed. Feels the warm September air waft through the open bedroom windows. Sees rays of the morning sunshine glance off his old dresser. Goes for the paper's sports section next.

Maris is busy beside him. She asked him to bring up a

wicker basket filled with denim placemats she'd been making for the new kitchen. After settling the basket beside the bed, she reaches for one of the placemats and a pair of sewing scissors. Her pillows are propped behind her as she leans against the headboard. The placemat is in her lap. Slowly, slowly, she works the scissors along the placemat's edge to clean up the stitched hem. There's only the soft sound of her trimming scissors *snip-snipping* random threads.

Jason's reading that sports section as she works. Leaning against the headboard, too, he's sitting with a knee up and the paper against it. He's halfway into some article about the contenders for the upcoming World Series. But he's doing something else, too. He's occasionally watching Maris. And worrying a little bit about her. Especially as he catches her trying to quell a slight shake in her hand. It happens when she's maneuvering the scissors around those denim placemats.

Still, he says nothing.

But after a few minutes, he can't help it. He silently reaches over and squeezes her trembling hand. Holds it for a long moment, too. Finally, he leans over and kisses the top of her head before getting back to his paper.

eleven

SOME DAYS, DEPENDING ON WHICH way the wind blows, Shane wakes up with a grimace. It happens on mornings when a sea breeze carries the foul scent of lobster bait—straight from the Rockport docks to his nearby little shingled house. Nothing like the pungent odor of old salted herring to get you sitting up pronto, then rushing to the window and closing it before grabbing another ten minutes of dozing.

Saturday's one of those days.

But he cuts short the dozing because he's off to Shiloh's brunch this morning. Shiloh's parents host the get-together once or twice a year before any big lobstering excursion. And Lord knows, Shane, Shiloh and the rest of the crew are damn well about to make up for seriously lost time. They've been off the water for two weeks now as the boat's busted fuel pump was being repaired. Captain gave the go-ahead and they're ready to return to sea Monday. So the brunch is a send-off with good wishes. Several of the town's lobster crews will be there, giving Shane a chance to catch up with the boys.

Now, thanks to a stinkin' salted-herring wake-up, Shane's showered and ready to hit the road. It's a cool morning, so he puts on a button-down over his tee and jeans, grabs his newsboy cap and heads out. Shiloh's place is inland a ways. Driving the winding roads, Shane passes shingled homes where front yards are stacked with lobster traps. He also notices the sugar maples along the coast are turning orange already. Fall's definitely a-comin'. Traffic's light, too; the tourists have dwindled this month.

Finally, he approaches a big piece of property where a stream of pickup trucks is turning into the side yard. Truck doors are slamming closed. Farm dogs trot around the arriving guests. Guys from various lobster crews mill around, call out. The American flag is blowing on a flagpole.

But it's the barn where everything's happening—and where everyone's heading. It's the last of two old barns once on the land. And when Shane turns *his* pickup in the side yard, there's no missing that the place is *fully* decorated for the event. A banner of flags—lobster flags and fishing vessel flags—is strung above the barn's open wooden doors. Inside the vaulted structure, clear illuminated bulbs hang from the rough-hewn rafters. Much catered food is spread over several tables below them. There are steaming trays of bacon, eggs, hash browns and biscuits. A fruit-and-yogurt bar to the side. Hell, there's a doughnut bar. And a juice bar—hard drinks and not. Baskets of bagels are scattered around. Cream cheeses, too. Vintage ship wheels are propped on the food tables. Old lobster traps are strewn here and there along the barn's planked walls. Garlands of twisted fishing rope loop across the table edges. There are tarnished lanterns scattered about; white-painted baskets are stuffed with utensils. Across long picnic tables, dishes are set out on burlap placemats; cloth napkins lying across the dishes are tied in seashell-threaded wire. More burlap is wrapped around clear jars filled with sand, stones and candles.

Oh, yes. When Shane walks into the barn, he knows. Shiloh's family is ready for some genuine Downeast revelry.

⌒

"Shane!" a man's voice calls out.

Shane turns to see Shiloh's parents approaching. They're middle-aged and dressed casual—he in a striped light sweater over jeans with rolled cuffs; she in a gray V-neck top over black Bermuda shorts. "Keith. Tammy," Shane says, giving them a hug.

"How've you been, Shane?" Keith asks while clapping Shane's shoulder. "Shiloh tells us he's seen you around town some these past couple of weeks."

"Ayuh. Here and there. And I'm good—thanks for asking." Shane lifts two bags he'd brought in. "Got something for you, Tammy."

"Shane!" She tucks back her shoulder-length silvery-blonde hair. "What is it?" she asks, taking the heavy bags from him then.

"Fresh tomatoes. Some special folk in Connecticut have themselves a beautiful sea garden. Air off Long Island Sound drifts over it. Salty mist douses the plants, too."

Keith takes a tomato out of one of the bags and eyes it closely.

"Now listen, Keith," Shane instructs him. "You go ahead and slice that up and tell me if it isn't the *finest* tomato you've ever tasted."

Keith does. Biting into a half-slice, his eyes drop closed as he murmurs, "*Wow.*" Then he slices several more on a nearby table. Tammy, meanwhile, sets out the plates of sweet tomato slices with dishes of mayo and shakers of sea salt for all the lobstermen to enjoy.

All the while, a few of the guys slap Shane's back. Call out rowdy greetings. One in particular gets his attention.

"There's the lovesick loser," Shiloh says when he walks into the barn.

"And there's the *loser*," Shane tells him back with a good shove. "How you doin', Shi?" he asks when they get in the buffet line. "Ready to quit globbin' around and hit the high seas?"

"Eh. Been a landlubber for a coupla weeks. Got to get my sea legs back now."

"It's like riding a bike," Shane assures him as they fill their plates with breakfast chow. Shane's scooping a serving of baked oatmeal with blueberries. "Sea legs come back as soon as your feet hit the deck."

"How 'bout you?" Shiloh asks minutes later when they're sitting at a picnic table with the other guys. "You got your head on straight, bub? Or is Celia taking up valuable real estate in that noggin of yours?"

Another shove or two ensues. And raucous small talk. Shane turns when someone slaps his shoulder. "Yo, Bradford," the guy says as he sets down his plate beside Shane and Shiloh. "Make room."

"Hey, Alex. Shit," Shane tells him, sliding over on the picnic table bench. "Every time you show up, *I* end up with a new tattoo."

"You're in luck," Alex tells him. "Keith and Tammy had me set up my kit on a special tattoo table outside."

"Might get one myself," Shiloh says, rolling up a shirtsleeve.

And as they deliberate tattoo designs, the barn quiets some. All the crews settle in with cinnamon rolls and scrambled eggs and toast and sausage. Powder-sugar-dusted waffles and popovers filled with fresh fruit. When Shane goes for seconds, Shiloh's mother pulls him aside.

"Listen, Shane," she says, leaning close. "Shiloh mentioned you bought him a really good fishing bib this week. One that was out of his budget. Over at MaineStay."

"I did, Tammy."

"Well, that was *nice* of you. But here," she says, trying to give him a fifty-dollar bill as he scoops a heap of scrambled eggs onto his plate. "Take this."

"Oh, no." Shane backs away and holds up an open hand. "My treat, Tammy. It's important Shiloh have the right gear out there on the Atlantic."

"But Shane—"

"No, I won't hear of it," Shane tells her when she tries again to push the money on him. "Your son's just going to have to really step it up on the boat now," he adds with a wink, then drops buttered toast on his dish.

Giving a warm smile, Tammy shakes her head. "You took Shiloh under your wing all those years ago when he started up on the boats."

"Five years now. Come a helluva long way from his greenhorn days."

"And we're well aware it's a dangerous racket out there, so … well, Keith and I appreciate it. All you've done for our boy."

"He's a good kid, Tammy. You two should be mighty proud of Shiloh. A real hard worker, he is. Twenty-six years old and keeping on the straight and narrow. No small feat." Shane tips his newsboy cap at her before turning back to the tables.

"Oh, Shane!" Tammy calls, catching up with him once more. "One more thing. Shiloh tells me and Keith you have a new lady in your life."

Shane nods. "Celia."

"Do you have a picture of her?"

"That I do." Shane sets down his dish, pulls his phone from his pocket and swipes through the photos there. He finally lands on one: Celia, chin resting on hand, while sitting at his shabby backyard table a week ago. Silver chains hang over her white tee. And she's watching him. He shows Tammy the picture.

"My goodness, she's beautiful." Tammy looks up from the photo. "And seems to only have eyes for you."

"She means a lot to me," he says while pocketing his phone.

"Well, if you two *ever* tie the knot, we've got a nice piece of land here for a barn wedding. They're all the rage, you know."

Shane gives a short laugh. "We're not there yet, Tammy. But you let Keith know that I'll keep that offer of yours in mind."

"Good!" Tammy scoops up a slice of pie and adds it to his plate. "And have some pie. That's blueberry. From Fiona's Farm."

"Much obliged, Tammy."

"Ma!" Shiloh wanders over from the tables. "What're you pestering Shane about now?"

"Oh, it's nothing. Just catching up some."

"Well, come on, Shane." Shiloh hitches his head. "Bets are getting laid down on the horseshoe games lining up for later."

"You and Shiloh grab more food while the gettin's good," Tammy calls, motioning to the tables. "Once Hunter and his crew come through here, there'll be *nothing* left in those tins."

⌇

Saturday morning in the hardware store, Cliff strides to the paint department. There's much on his to-do list today, but this paint issue tops it. Curls of old paint are lifting off the guard shack as it is. Not to mention, complaints about the shack's neglected appearance have been issued to the Board of Governors. So Cliff stands at the paint counter with samples in hand. Nick told him the two he's between, and Cliff added a few more colors from the paint chip aisle. He'll just put in his order for those peel-and-stick, eight-by-eight color swatches and be on his way.

"Doing some fixin' up, Clifton?" a man asks from behind him. "Painting a room in your house?"

Cliff turns to see Mitch Fenwick. He's standing there munching on the hardware store's complimentary popcorn stuffed into a paper cone. "Painting?" Cliff asks back, then looks at the paint chips he's holding. "Well, no. I mean, yes. But not my house. It's that guard shack that needs some sprucing up." Cliff fans out the chips to show them all. "And you, Mitchell? What brings you here today?"

"Making a copy of my cottage key." He lifts a tarnished key from his safari-style shirt pocket and holds it up. "For the construction workers at my place. With school back in session, I'm at the college teaching more often now and can't always let them in."

Cliff nods. "Makes sense. So ... well okay, then," he says, turning to get back in line at the paint counter. "I'll be on my way now."

In a moment, Cliff's up next at the counter and he steps forward—but stops. Stops and spins—yes, *spins*—back around. "Actually, I don't typically do this," he calls after Mitch veering off, "but I have to right now." Customers in line *behind* Cliff shift. And look past him to the waiting clerk at the counter. Some turn up their hands. "Would you mind coming here, Mitchell? To the paint chip row?" Cliff asks, abruptly stepping out of that line and heading that way himself.

"Over yonder?" Mitch asks around a mouthful of popcorn. "Why, sure. Need a second opinion?"

Cliff glances back at him. "Yeah. Something like that." He says no more until Mitch catches up to him at the racks filled with rows and rows of paint chips. Cliff slowly turns one of those racks as though he's perusing the various colors. "We need to talk, man to man," he's also saying to Mitch beside him—while lifting another paint chip from the rack, too. "So, I'll begin by telling you I'd appreciate it if you'd just ... lay off."

Mitch is still munching popcorn. While he chews, he's got one hand scooping out more from the cone. "Now," he says to Cliff, "I have the feeling you're *not* talking about paint chips here."

"You'd be right, too. I'm talking about *Elsa*. Because …
look. I know something's going on between you two," Cliff
says, pointing one of those chips directly at Mitch.

"I won't deny that."

"But listen. Maybe *you're* not aware of something."

"And what's that?"

"I've been *seeing* Elsa DeLuca for a year now," Cliff tells
him. "We have a lot of history together at Stony Point.
Emotional history. And really? You don't know diddly-squat
about what Elsa and I have been through."

Mitch drags a hand down his goatee. "Here's the thing,
Cliff. I *like* you," he says, pointing that popcorn cone
toward Cliff. "Got no beef with you, actually. You were
kind to my daughter, Carol, that night a few weeks back
when you helped maneuver that *massive* ice-cream cake up
to my deck. And … and you helped rescue Gordon's lost
rowboat. So I would *normally* count you as one of my *friends*,
man," Mitch says, tossing a few popcorn kernels in his
mouth. "But, uh, we're not *in* a normal situation here, are
we?"

"Guess there's no dancing around the subject anymore,
Mitchell. It's practically the elephant on the beach that no
one's mentioning."

"It is." Mitch crumples his empty popcorn cone. "And
you're right, Cliff. I don't know your history with Elsa. But
what I *do* know is this." He motions for Cliff to wait as he
tosses that crumpled paper cone in a trash can over by the
paint counter. "I *know*," Mitch continues then without
missing a beat, "that Elsa's made it *very* clear she's not
committed to any *one* person right now. The lady simply is
not spoken for—"

"But she *is*," Cliff interrupts. "That's what I'm trying to tell you right now."

"Well, that's not what Elsa's telling me. So … *you're* not going to decide who she'll see. And *I'm* not going to decide either. The beautiful Mrs. DeLuca is going to decide. And she *is* pretty as a peach. Smart as all get-out, too. She'll make up her mind in her own sweet time. Oh," Mitch says before turning away, "and one more thing."

"What now?" Cliff asks, tapping his several paint chips in his open hand.

"Well." Mitch pauses and rubs his goatee again while squinting at those paint chips. "Think you might go a shade darker on that paint color," he says, pointing to the blues Cliff holds. "Samples there look a little weak."

"*What?*" Cliff glances from Mitch to the paint chips.

Mitch gives another nod and slight salute. "Now you have a good day, Commissioner."

"Professor," Cliff answers, then turns in the opposite direction—toward the paint counter—but gives one quick glance over his shoulder as he does.

⌒

Kyle grabs onto the doorframe and leans into the Dockside Diner's kitchen. It's early afternoon already and he wants to get going. "Jerry?" he asks. "You're not just saying it, right? You're *really* good to take over here the rest of the day?"

"You got it," Jerry tells him from the big stove. Hamburgers and sandwiches are sizzling there all at once— the burgers cooking; the sandwiches toasting beneath a cast-iron grill press. "I'll keep the customers fed and lock up later. *You* go keep folks fed at the Barlows'." He looks over his shoulder at Kyle. "You got enough to go around?"

"Yeah." Kyle considers the containers at his feet. "Got the coolers. Heating trays. Insulated bags," he says, stacking the trays on the final cooler, then looping the insulated bags over his arm. "Call you later. You're the best, Jer!" Kyle yells on his way to the diner's rear door. He shoulders it open and walks outside into bright September sunshine. His new pickup is already backed to the loading dock, so he carefully fills it with the goods. But after closing the truck tailgate, he stops before leaving and leans against the diner's outside wall. It's been a busy Saturday here, with a steady turnout of customers. The outdoor patio off to the side is jumping. Bags of water and copper pennies hanging from low tree branches there catch his eye, too. Sunshine reflecting off the shiny pennies deflects bugs, keeping away the pesky yellow jackets that would otherwise be bothering his outdoor patrons this time of year.

"*All's good*," Kyle quietly says, taking his cell phone from his pants pocket and making a call. Seconds later, someone picks up.

"Yo, bro," Shane says.

"Shane. Sup with you?" As he asks, Kyle hears voices in the background from wherever Shane might be. Rowdy voices, hootin' and hollerin'. "Got a minute?"

"Just one. I'm at a barn brunch for the lobster crews. One of the families puts this shindig on every year."

"*Come on, Bradford*," a voice calls in the distance—Kyle can't miss it. "*You're up next*."

"That's Alex," Shane tells Kyle. "Dude always shows up

at these things with his tattoo kit. So I'm about to get inked again on my arm. Got one guy ahead of me."

"What'll the tat be this time?"

"Still mulling it over," Shane lets on. "But hey, aren't you working? Lunchtime on a Saturday? Must be busy as hell there."

"Yeah, it is. But Jerry's manning the stoves the rest of the day."

"Uh-oh. And you're wasting time calling me? Spill it, bro. What happened?"

Kyle lifts a foot to the wall he leans against and does just that. Spills his story. Tells Shane about Maris' near-miss deer-collision. And how afterward he went with Jason to deliver Maris' car to the dealer. She'd left it roadside as Jason got her home. Kyle answers Shane's concerned questions, too. His, *Maris okay?* And his, *The deer make it?* And lastly, *The car wrecked?*

"No, everything dodged the bullet. The car, the deer. But I think it was a closer call than Jason and Maris are letting on. Shit, were they plenty shook up."

"No kidding."

"Yeah. And ... you know. They've had a bitch of a month already. So I'm *really* going to show up for them today."

"How so, man?"

"Hell, lots of friends are stopping by to check on Maris. So I'll keep everyone fed while the Barlows are busy with guests." Kyle pushes off the wall and heads to his pickup now. "But they really went through some wringer yesterday, Shane. Wanted to let you know."

"Appreciate it."

"No prob. I'm on my way to the Barlows' now. And you enjoy that brunch going down," Kyle tells him after climbing in his truck and closing the door. "Oh hey, guy. Take care of yourself on the water, too. You hear me?"

twelve

OKAY, THAT'S ANOTHER HOUR TO log." As he says it, Jason reaches to his nightstand for the depleted hourglass and flips it over. Picks up his architectural-journal-turned-lost-time-recovered log and jots in the past hour's details, too. *"Contemplating new photo for Ted's picture frame,"* he whispers, his pen jotting the words.

Maris looks up from the photos on Jason's phone and lifts the empty picture frame off the mattress. The frame is made with weathered and distressed planks of wood. A silver boat cleat is mounted *beneath* the space for a photograph, that cleat a nautical accent. Ted Sullivan gave Jason the frame for a wedding gift, and the frame's still empty. Maris sets it beside a half-eaten lunch sandwich on her own nightstand. "I can't believe we've had that frame for two years now."

"I know. So let's decide on a picture for it." Sitting beside Maris on the bed, Jason leans against the pillows propped against the headboard, takes his phone back and scrolls the photos.

Maris leans over to see, then looks toward the window. "Even with that fan on, it's still getting warm in here, don't you think?"

"Little bit. Here." Jason sets aside his phone and stretches past her for an elastic on her nightstand. "Let me braid your hair," he says, motioning her to turn around. "I'll get it off your neck."

"You will?" When he nods, she touches his scruffy jaw. "I'm loving this day, Jason. Just having this quiet time with you. No one around. Just relaxing together."

"So am I, sweetheart."

After lightly kissing him, Maris turns, sits cross-legged and lifts all her hair back, dropping it behind her shoulders. "Good?" she asks.

"Yeah." Sitting behind her, Jason starts loosely separating hair sections. "You keep scrolling through the pictures," his low voice says while his fingers entwine her hair. "Pick your favorite."

Maris is quiet then. While feeling Jason's fingers separate and twist and touch wide strands of her hair, she browses the photographs on his phone. Then hers. Then back to his. She also gets drowsy with the sensation of his fingers lifting and moving strands of her hair. That sensation's unknotting her shoulder muscles. Her neck. The warm salt air drifting in and brushing her skin makes it more than she can take. Her eyelids feel heavy.

"I keep coming back to this picture," she finally says. It's a close-up of her and Jason sitting side by side on sand chairs on the beach. In the bright sunshine, her navy tankini's deep-V top shows as she leans against Jason's bare, wet shoulder. Their drenched hair is slicked back; seawater drips from their faces. Maris touches the image, then holds the phone up so he can see it behind her. "It's from our beach day—two weeks ago already."

"I like that one."

"Me, too." Again she looks at the picture. "Because it's just a moment, Jason. An unplanned, easy moment. Like the ones we're trying to recover now."

"Especially today," Jason says as he secures her long braid with the elastic. "You stay put, I'll be right back," he tells her then, first grabbing that half-eaten sandwich of hers—which he finishes in two bites—before going downstairs. When he returns, it's with his laptop.

Together now, they lean against the headboard. Maris sits close beside him. She points to the picture as he manipulates it in his photo app. "Crop there. A little more," she adds as Jason edits the photograph on his computer. "*Yes!* Perfect," she tells him when the crop is done and the horizon straightened. "I love it. That one moment."

"Okay. So wait here."

"Where are you going?"

Jason closes his laptop, gets off the bed and puts on the work boots he'd meant to do yard work in. "I'll print this right now. In my barn studio. That way? We can finally get a picture into that frame," he says before turning to leave.

"All right, babe." As she says it, Maris slinks down on the bed. "And I feel really sleepy now. So I'm actually going to take a little nap—something I haven't done in ages."

Jason turns back from the hallway and leans into the

bedroom. "I'll join you in ten minutes. Save me a spot on that bed."

⁓

Jason takes Maddy with him to his barn studio in the backyard. Afternoon sunlight streams in through the double sliders and the skylights there. Maddy drops right into a pool of that warm light while Jason turns on the professional printer he uses for work. In no time, the unit clicks and whirrs as the glossy photo he'd sent it emerges on the tray. He also takes a few minutes to thumb through a pile of unopened mail on his big desk. There are bills and design flyers. Some payments came in on customer invoices, too. After opening those, he sets it all aside to put his newly printed photograph in a folder before heading back to the house.

But a surprise comes as he opens the double-slider screen and sees that Kyle just arrived. He's standing at his pickup's bed and lifting out coolers and assorted prep and serving gear. So Jason whistles for the dog and heads out, leaving the studio door half open so Maddy can catch up.

"Yo, Barlow," Kyle calls out when he catches sight of him approaching.

"Kyle." Jason walks to the truck. He also notices that Kyle's still in his chef getup: black tee and black pants. "What are you doing here again? Shouldn't you be behind the big stove, guy?"

"Jerry's got it covered." Kyle hefts another large cooler from the truck. "I'm taking care of my best man and his wife this afternoon. Brought a whole spread," he calls back to Jason as he climbs the deck stairs.

"What?"

"Got any extra tables, dude? Some folding tables, maybe?" Kyle asks as he sets the heavy cooler on the deck and looks around. He turns back to Jason still in the driveway. "Some camping tables in the shed?"

"I do, actually. But why?"

Kyle leans on the splintery deck railing and talks to Jason down below. "Figured people would be in and out of here all day. Might as well feed them." He squints at Jason climbing the stairs now. "You're certainly not leaving that bedroom ... to *host*."

"Kyle, get real." Jason keeps climbing the stone steps. "People are *busy*. They have better things to do on a Saturday than hang out here."

"Maybe. But Lauren's upstairs right now." Once Jason's on the deck, Kyle heads down the stairs for what looks like heating trays and insulated bags of prepared food. "I sent her in the front door."

Jason looks up toward his gabled cottage's second floor, then back down at Kyle in the driveway now. "You kidding me?" he asks.

"No way, man. So grab me some small tables and I'll set up." Kyle hoists more diner gear into his arms. "Oh. And I need an extension cord, too. For the hot plates."

"You really don't have to do this," Jason says. He looks at the photo folder he's still holding, then down to Kyle in the driveway—right as Kyle's lifting a tote strap onto his shoulder. "It's too much trouble, guy," Jason calls to him. "And I *doubt* anyone else is coming by. Maris talked to them all last night!"

Kyle nods to the long driveway running beside the

house. "And here we go," he says, then turns to carry his gear up the deck stairs.

From up on the deck, Jason squints past him to the driveway—only to see Celia walking up it. She's wearing a loose tee and faded cuffed shorts while pushing Aria's stroller, too.

⌒⌣

Huh, Kyle was right.

By the time Jason gets the camping tables from the shed; and a folding table from the back of the garage; *and* brings the printed photograph back up to Maris in the bedroom … it's begun.

En masse.

When Jason turns into his upstairs bedroom, Lauren is sitting on the bed. She's wearing a belted maxi dress and is leaning against the headboard—*and* holding Aria. Celia's sitting cross-legged on the foot of the bed. She's dipping a brush into a nail polish bottle, then taking hold of one of Lauren's bare feet and painting her nails. As she paints, she's telling Lauren and Maris about her trip to Addison today. Jason stands there in the doorway and takes it all in—because there's more. Maris is bent over *her* folded knees and diligently painting her own toenails. Her long brown braid hangs forward over her shoulder. Someone also turned on the crank-up radio on Jason's dresser. So music is playing over all the fan-blowing and nail-polishing and baby-holding and chattering.

Just then, Maris looks up from her polishing. "*Jason!*" She puts the brush in the polish bottle. "Lauren stopped in with nail polish for some fun girl time—and found me *napping*! I mean … I was *sound asleep*! Couldn't you have given me some notice?"

"How was I to—"

"Didn't Kyle tell you?" Lauren cuts him off while running a finger through wisps of Aria's hair.

"Well, yeah. But …" Jason walks into the room—his work boots clomping across the hardwood floor—and gets the empty picture frame from Maris' nightstand. "I was printing out your photograph, sweetheart," he explains, finagling it into the frame.

"Ooh, let's see it," Celia says from the end of the bed.

Jason holds up the now-framed glossy picture of him and Maris dripping wet on the beach.

"Aw. Look Aria!" Lauren turns the baby in her lap. "You guys are so cute," she tells Jason.

"And you Barlows better stay together now," Celia warns, waggling a finger.

Jason nods. "So I got that printed," he says while walking across the room. "Then Kyle wrangled me into hauling folding camp tables out of the shed. Maris, do you know he brought a whole spread for our visitors?"

"Spread?" Maris asks, dabbing her toenails again.

Jason sets their framed photo beside the radio on his dresser. "There's an appetizer *feast* out there," he's saying while straightening the frame. "Coolers of this, hot tins of that, you name it."

"It's the diner to-go for you guys today," Lauren tells them.

"*Babe*," Maris insists. "You better bring me up some!"

"I will," Jason says. "Later. Kyle's just setting up."

And as Celia fans Lauren's nails now; and as Maris dabs

another coat of polish on her toes; and as Aria coos and laughs with the ladies, Lauren leans back against the headboard again. "You know something? You guys have the right idea," she says, lightly bouncing Aria in her lap. "Hanging out in bed all day."

"Yeah." Jason shuts off the radio, crosses his arms and leans against the dresser. "It *was* a good idea—until my bed got hijacked."

"Jason! They wanted to check up on me," Maris explains, setting her nail polish bottle on the nightstand. "We have the *best* friends. Come on!"

"Wait," Celia says from where she still sits on the end of the bed. She turns toward one of the open windows. "Is someone here? I thought I heard a car door slam."

"I'll go see." Lauren leans forward and scoots little Aria into Celia's cross-legged lap. "I have to call my parents anyway and touch base with them. They're watching Hailey and Ev," Lauren tells them when she stands and straightens her maxi dress. She walks around the bed and hugs Maris, too. "I'm *so* glad you didn't even get a scratch, girlfriend."

"Me, too," Maris agrees. "You coming back up?"

"I might go see Kyle on the deck for a while." Lauren blows her a kiss. Then Celia, the baby and Jason get one, too. They all wave Lauren off as she leaves the bedroom and hurries downstairs.

Problem is, in only *seconds*, Jason hears the door open and another familiar voice talking.

"What's shakin'?" Nick's voice is asking Lauren.

Lauren must've taken a few steps back to the staircase then. "Hey guys! Nick's here," she calls out. "I'm sending him up!"

"*Upstairs?*" Nick asks her. "Really?"

When Lauren answers, "Yes! Everyone's there," Jason walks to a window, moves aside the sheer curtain and catches sight of Kyle on the back deck. He's still setting up his hot plates and tins of food.

Good thing, because not only does Nick come rolling into the bedroom now, but Maddy does, too. The German shepherd stops right at Celia and sniffs at the cooing baby in her lap, all while Nick's talking to Maris.

"Hey, there's the woman of the hour. Feeling better today?" he asks while giving Maris a side hug. "We were so worried about you!"

"Thanks, I'm okay," Maris says into the slight hug.

"Good, good!" When Nick straightens, Jason can't miss the way he looks around at the blowing fan, and at Celia and the baby, and at Jason. Then Nick takes in the newspaper sections, the radio, the denim placemats, nail polish. "So ... What's going on here?"

"Oh, they'll fill you in," Celia says, touching Aria's fingers to Maddy's soft ears, then standing with the cooing baby. "I'm on my way out. This little one needs her afternoon nap." As she says it, she cradles Aria to her shoulder and turns to the door.

"Thanks for stopping by," Maris calls to her.

"Kyle brought a ton of food," Jason says, looking from Kyle outside to Celia. "Be sure to come back later."

"If it means I don't have to cook?" she asks, winking at Maris. "I definitely will. And Kyle's food is always the bomb. Save me a plate, guys?"

"Will do," Jason assures her. "So long as the vultures don't down it first."

"There's *food* out back?" Nick looks out the window where Jason's standing, so Jason heads to his bedside chair and sits there. "Maris?" Nick asks, turning to her. "I'm glad you're doing good. But I'm on my lunch hour, so I want to grab some chow from Kyle."

Maris gives Nick a friendly shoo. "Go for it."

When he leaves, Jason unlaces and takes off his work boots first. Then he semi-straightens his side of the bedcover in the finally quiet room. After lying down on the mattress, he just closes his eyes and breathes. That's it. In a moment, he also feels Maris' feather touch to his arm as she strokes the skin there.

"*The best-laid plans* ..." her soft voice nearly whispers.

"Oh, we should've known," Jason answers, his voice as quiet as hers. Now he tosses an arm across his closed eyes. "I'm going to steal ten peaceful minutes here while I can."

Suddenly a loud rap sounds on the front door downstairs.

"Barlow?" Matt's voice calls out seconds later.

thirteen

WELL, NOW. LATE THAT AFTERNOON, Elsa's a little taken aback.

She *thought* she'd have a nice, easy visit with Maris.

Not *this*.

Not that she'd be *vying* for Maris' attention. Good heavens, there must be a *crowd* here—gauging by the vehicles parked willy-nilly in the Barlow driveway. Elsa recognizes Kyle's spiffy new truck, near the deck. And Lauren's car, too. It looks like Nick's security cruiser is pulled over on the grass. Then Matt's here. And wait—is that *Cliff's* car behind Matt's?

Shaking her head, Elsa carefully steers her golf cart onto the grass closer to Jason's barn studio. After parking and dropping the key in her straw tote, she removes the silky scarf from around her freshly dyed hair. Lightly waggles out that scarf and ties it to the handle of her driver's seat, too. Who'd have thought there'd be a big bash going on? That's what it seems like—what with the chattering and laughing voices up on the deck. And are those smoking *grills*? Or hot plates? Lord knows, Kyle's tending to *something* cooking up there. The patio umbrella is open, too. Lauren's setting out dishes on the table.

But still … no sign of Maris among everyone mingling about.

From her parked golf cart, Elsa keeps looking, this time around the yard. There's Maddy's kiddie pool—filled with clear water, but no dog. So she looks *past* the pool to Jason's barn studio. Weathered fishing buoys hang randomly on its brown, rough-hewn walls.

But no Maris in sight.

Unless …

As Elsa reaches for a gift basket from the passenger seat, she notices something. The double doors to that barn studio are half open. So after getting out of the golf cart, she brings the gift she brought for Maris that way. With no sign of Maris *or* Jason on the deck with the others, maybe they're in the studio.

"*Time to find out*," Elsa tells herself, passing an old, dried-out lobster trap propped near the open studio doors. Carefully, she pushes the screen door open a little more and steps inside the barn. Rays of sunlight drop through the skylights. "Jason?" she calls out, glancing around. There's not a sign of life here. "Maris?" she asks, turning toward a wall of massive framed photographs. Each one depicts one of Jason's redesigned beach cottages and seaside homes. She stops in front of the framed Ocean Star Inn and actually sighs. There in front of her are the inn's stone walls and the shingled structure with its turret and porches. Jason did an

99

unbelievable job renovating the place. All the property's original architectural integrity was well honored—but brought completely up-to-date in the New England coastal aesthetic. Now if she could only get the inn opened.

"*Oh!*" she says, waving off the photograph and turning away. She walks past Jason's drafting table with its swing-arm lamp—all while muffled voices carry into the barn from out on the Barlow deck. Someone *must* have been in the studio. Otherwise, the doors would never be left open like they were. Elsa stops at the bottom of the stairs leading to the loft. "Maris?" she asks, holding the railing and looking up the stairs. "It's me. *Elsa.*"

No response.

But Elsa pauses there and waits—just in case Maris comes running around a corner. Or leans over the railing to call out a happy hello.

Instead there's just the big old moose head silently watching Elsa from its mount at the top of the staircase wall. The moose's antlers spread wide as its glassy gaze peers down its long brown nose. There's some mysterious story about how that moose head ended up here. Something about it being stolen from Foley's, back in the day.

But alas, no Maris. Anywhere.

So Elsa heads back outside with her gift basket. She's sure to close the screen door but doesn't lock it up. Jason must've left it open for *some* reason. So she only lightly closes the slider. Looking across the lawn dappled with afternoon sunlight, she heads in the direction of the deck next. And in no time at all, she's sucked into a vortex of chaos.

⌒⌣

Happy chaos.

People wander here and there. Greetings float Elsa's way. A hug does, too, from Lauren. Vinny and Paige are just arriving. More hugs. Kyle's manning the hot plates. It looks like he's heating up grilled chicken tortillas. Spicy chicken wings, too. And bacon cheeseburger sliders. Appetizers of all kinds are sizzling. The works.

But there's no Maris to be found.

In full guard uniform, Nick's leaning against the deck railing and sipping a cold drink, so Elsa walks over. "Nicholas? Aren't you working?"

Nick nods. "Still on the clock, actually. Had lunch here earlier, and swung by now to be sure no ordinances are being broken before my shift's up."

Elsa half listens while still looking around. "But where's Maris?"

"Upstairs," Nick says, raising his glass toward the gabled house's second floor. "In bed."

"*What?*" Elsa twists around and looks up at the second-floor windows, then spins back to Nick. "Is she under the weather? You know, having some aches and pains from her almost-accident?"

"Hardly," Matt assures Elsa as he joins Nick with a bottle of beer in hand. "Go have a look," he says, motioning Elsa to the kitchen slider.

"Well. I think I will." She carries her gift basket in that direction, but turns back toward Matt. "Is Eva up there? Keeping Maris company?"

"No. She's showing a house. But she'll be here later, I'm sure."

"Oh. Okay." Elsa opens the slider to the stunning new

kitchen and crosses the room. It's actually quieter in the house than it is outside. In the hallway past the kitchen, voices come to her from upstairs. Or rather, *a* voice. It's Maris talking. So Elsa hurries to the staircase, but stops at the bottom.

The night is black as can be, she hears Maris say. *What makes it even blacker is the calm.*

One careful step at a time, Elsa climbs the stairs leading up to the bedrooms—and she listens, too, catching phrases of Maris' tale.

She plays a game of cat and mouse with the sea. She steps close, then hurries backward as another wave reaches for her ... He joins her, and they stand side by side. When they squint into the darkness at the rising black sea, he feels her hand slip into his. The next wave is bigger.

At the top landing, Elsa actually stops and listens more. Maris is still talking. Or ... she could be reading. Her voice comes steady as she's telling some story.

"Let's go!" he shouts, still holding her hand. He hitches his head to the cottage-on-stilts behind them. The cottage is dark, too. With its windows boarded, they can't even make out the candlelight inside.

Maris' serious tone intrigues Elsa, so she tiptoes toward the bedroom—Maris' voice still talking. And Elsa realizes now that what she's hearing is actually a passage from Maris and Neil's novel, *Driftline.*

When another wave splashes too close, Maris goes on, *and too violently now, she only squeezes his hand.*

At the bedroom's open doorway, Elsa stops. She silently looks in. The room's a bit of a mess. There's a sloppy pile of newspaper sections at the foot of the bed. A basket of some sewing project is on the floor. Scissors and pieces of faded and distressed denim spill from the basket. Maris' nightstand is covered with nail polish bottles and two coffee cups and a crumb-covered plate. There's a random radio and framed photograph propped on a dresser. Jason's pewter hourglass is on *his* nightstand along with some journal and pens and a deck of cards and glass of water. .There's an open box of chocolates there, too. Beat-up work boots are on the floor near a chair.

And then there's Jason—lying on the bed in an old college tee and cargo shorts. An arm's crooked over his eyes as *he* listens to Maris. She's half-lying in some olive-colored lounge pants and top. She's barefoot, too, and holding her papers against a propped knee. A pedestal fan is blowing steady on her and Jason. They're both completely engrossed in what she's reading.

There's something wild and free about the storm's stealth as it inches closer. It gets her dark hair blowing; his shirt whips in that wind.

"Let's stay," she says.

And Elsa knows, watching her niece and Jason intimately reading and listening. They're lying so low after a really close call yesterday. And what it does, seeing the two of them lounging on that bed, is this: It shows Elsa how very serious the near-accident actually was—*and* what was on the line to be lost.

"*Maris,*" Elsa whispers now while standing in the doorway.

Maris looks up from her manuscript papers and straightens from her lounging position on the bed. At the same time, Jason lifts his arm from his eyes and squints across the casually messy bedroom to Elsa. His dark hair is wavy; his face, covered with scruffy whiskers.

"What'd you think of that passage, Elsa?" he asks, then sits up against the headboard.

Before she can answer, tears fill Elsa's eyes. But still, she's frozen in the doorway. "*It's beautiful,*" she manages to say, her voice closing up on her. "Of course I want to know what happens next."

"Okay!" Maris sets her manuscript pages on the nightstand and drops a brass ship-wheel paperweight on them. "You were so right, Jason. Mapping scenes on that big whiteboard of yours really helped," she continues, propping a pillow behind her.

"I use that whiteboard for quick cottage sketches all the time—talking out ideas with clients," Jason explains. "So don't go stealing it on me."

"Can I keep it in the shack a *few* more days? In case I still have to tinker with the scene?"

"No. No, tinkering. That scene's *perfect,*" Elsa insists, then swipes away a few escaped tears. She rushes to Maris, too. Oh, there's no stopping her as she first sets that gift basket on Maris' dresser, then practically *runs* to the bedside. There are no more words from Elsa. None from Maris, either. There's only a hug. One long, close embrace as Elsa bends to her niece and just about takes all of her up in her arms. And sways some. And squeezes her eyes shut while holding tight. When she finally manages to open her eyes—still hugging—Elsa notices Jason there on the bed beside Maris. He's simply watching them in their emotional moment. So Elsa reaches out one hand—which Jason takes and squeezes.

"It could've been real bad," he says to Elsa as she pulls

back from hugging Maris. "Yesterday. Could've had a whole different outcome." He stands then, straightens the cover on his side of the bed and pats it. "So sit with your niece," he tells her with a nod, then heads to one of the open windows. "Wait," he goes on, glancing back at Elsa—then twisting around to *try* to see the side yard out the window. "Is someone actually cutting my *hedges?*"

"What?" Maris asks.

Jason rushes to his bedside chair and puts on those dingy-looking work boots there. "I'll go monitor what's going on downstairs," he's saying while tying the laces. Once he's clomping down the hallway, he calls back, "And Elsa? You hang out with Maris!"

"Don't mind if I do," Elsa softly says. She takes her gift basket and sits on the bed with her niece. "I'm so happy to see you," she tells her while brushing back a wisp of hair fallen from Maris' braid.

"Me, too," Maris says.

And Elsa does stay there, just like Jason ordered. She and Maris sit against that bed's headboard and fluff the pillows. Once settled comfortably, Elsa hands over the gift basket she'd been holding. "For you," she tells Maris.

"Aunt Elsa! That's so thoughtful." Maris digs in the tissue paper spilling from that gift basket and pulls out a painted tin sun. Wavy sunrays extend from its center. Varying golden hues of metallic paint cover that entire tin sun—a beautiful sight, indeed.

"For your writing shack, maybe?" Elsa suggests. "Or somewhere on the deck?"

Maris runs her fingers over the painted tin. "It's *gorgeous.*"

Elsa nods, watching her sweet niece. "I picked that up at the farm stand because ... Well, because it just felt like the sun's shining a little brighter today," she says, then whispers the rest when Maris looks over at her. *"Knowing that you're okay."*

〜

And everything feels okay to Maris just then, too.

Sitting there with her aunt, she hears all the voices talking out on the deck. The laughs. Sunlight glances in through the sheer curtains and fills the bedroom. Salt air does, too. Maris admires Elsa's freshly cut-and-dyed hair. When she does, Elsa gets up to fuss with her hair at Maris' dresser mirror. All the while, that sound of hedge clippers trimming the bushes rises to the bedroom.

"Let me have a look-see at who the heck's cutting those hedges," Elsa says, veering off to an open window. She pushes aside the curtain and squints down toward the side yard, beyond the deck. "Seriously? It's Cliff!" She glances back at Maris over her shoulder. "Cliff's up on the ladder and cutting your hedges! I can see him over the top of them."

"Oh, yeah. Cliff came up here a little while ago." Maris stretches across the bed to Jason's nightstand. "Brought me this box of chocolates," she says, settling back against the headboard. "Jason and I killed much of them, but ..." She holds the box out toward Elsa.

"Cliff brought these?" Elsa asks, taking a chocolate from the box before returning to that window.

"Mm-hmm."

While nibbling the candy, Elsa moves aside that sheer

106

curtain and watches Cliff at the hedges again. In a moment, her hand goes to her heart.

"Cliff's been really great," Maris goes on. "He mowed the lawn while Jason was away at Ted Sullivan's, too."

"That must've been a big help." Elsa looks over at Maris, then out the window again. "Now Vinny's raking up the trimmings *behind* Cliff!"

"*Vinny?* He's here?"

"Paige, too. I saw her in the driveway when I pulled in."

"*Really?*" Maris stretches over to get a glimpse out the window. "I mean, Jason texted his sister this morning to tell her what happened with the deer. But they didn't have to come out here. I'm fine."

"Well, they did come. And Vinny's lending Cliff a hand."

"That's super nice of them, but honestly? *Jason* can do that yard stuff now. They should just kick back."

"Oh! And Celia's coming up. With the baby!"

"She *is?*" Maris looks up from the chocolates she's still perusing. "Cee was here earlier," Maris adds, lifting a candy to her mouth. "But she did say she'd pop by for dinner." Maris leans back and enjoys that creamy chocolate. Listens to the racket outside, too—the hedge trimmers and voices. Cliff calling to Vinny; Jason calling to Cliff; Lauren and Paige cooing over Aria; someone's cell phone ringing.

"Listen." Elsa turns from the window. "I better go downstairs and see what Celia's up to."

Right then, footsteps sound on the stairs outside the bedroom and Taylor rushes in. She's wearing a beige smocked tank top with a flouncy hem over really faded cutoffs and mule-sneakers. The teen's a *blur* of motion— her blonde hair flying behind her—as she runs to Maris.

"*Oh my gosh*, Auntie Maris! Uncle Jason sent me up here. How *are* you?" she asks into a quick hug. "You gave me and Mom a *huge* scare."

It's obvious that Taylor didn't even see Elsa at the window. When Maris looks at her past Taylor, Elsa's giving her a silent finger-wave and slipping out the bedroom door. So Maris turns to Taylor sitting on the edge of the mattress. "I'm so glad you're here," Maris tells her as she gets up off the bed.

"But I can only stay for, like, ten minutes. I'm on my way to Alison's for a movie marathon."

"Okay, sweetie. We'll have to hurry, then. Now you know you've got some great style—which, I love that top, by the way. So help me put together an outfit?"

"An outfit?" Taylor stands and sweeps her long blonde hair back over her shoulder. "For what?"

"Entertaining." Maris motions to the olive jogger set she's wearing. "It's time I get out of this bedroom and go downstairs with my guests." Maris motions Taylor to the walk-in closet across the room. "Let's check out my clothes. Your pick."

~⌒~

A promise is a promise, and Elsa's good for her word.

With Celia here, now's the time to keep her promise to Concetta—whose words stayed with Elsa ever since she got her friend's email last night. *Do not let one more day go by without reaching out to Celia.* And Elsa *promised* her she wouldn't. Problem is, the hours of this day *are* quickly passing—which means now's the time to reach out.

So as Elsa wanders the busy Barlow deck and watches the commotion brought on by Maris' near-accident, she gets an idea. Because though everyone's talking, and hot plates are smoking, and people are eating Kyle's assorted appetizers, there's an undercurrent of urgency to the whole atmosphere. A slight tension. And there shouldn't be tension because all's well with the Barlows. Crisis averted.

Which leads Elsa to her idea—one that needs backup.

That needs Celia.

Elsa finds her holding a plate of barbecued chicken wings at the far railing. Aria is strapped to her chest in a sling as Celia digs into one of those saucy wings. She'd changed into a striped tee and skinny jeans; her hair is down; and she waves to Elsa as she approaches.

Aria's all smiles now, too. She's facing out in that sling and squirms as Elsa nears.

"*Hello there, little love,*" Elsa coos to the baby. She also cradles her head and leaves a kiss on Aria's soft cheek. "Celia," she says then with a glance behind her first. She takes Celia's arm, too. "Would you help me with something?"

Celia sets down her plate and wipes her fingers on a napkin. "I'm listening," she tells Elsa.

That's enough of a *Yes* for Elsa. So she tugs Celia over to a shady spot on the deck corner and leans close. And talks quickly, but quietly. This is it. Because Elsa knows Concetta was right. If she fixes things with Celia, she'll have clarity on the rest of her dilemmas. And oh, does she need that clarity.

Which gets her to bridge the gap with Celia, right then and there.

"*To mend fences,*" Elsa cautiously begins, "I'd like to start fresh and get our business partnership back on track. And I have an idea." She reaches forward and squeezes Celia's hand. "I just don't want people to overhear." Elsa looks past her to the crowded deck. "So here goes ..." She leans close and spills it all, but stops after voicing her plan.

Stops at the sight of Celia nodding.

Nodding *and* agreeing to her impromptu plan.

Without hesitation, Celia also reaches around Aria strapped to her chest and manages to hug Elsa.

"*Okay*, then." Elsa steps back with a deep breath. "Let's begin?" When Celia nods again, Elsa spins around seeking out Jason. She hurries over to where he stands with Kyle at the mini stoves. While talking, Jason's got one hand cupped beneath a juicy cheeseburger slider in the other. And he devours that dripping little cheeseburger snack in two bites. "*Jason!*" Elsa says in a hushed and serious tone as she grabs his arm. "Give me a whistle."

"Oh, man." Jason wipes his hands on a paper napkin. "Every time I do this, my blood pressure rises with some announcement you make."

"That's right. And this is *important*." Elsa leans close to him. "So just do it."

Never one to let her down, Jason first turns up his hands in defeat. Then? He does it. He brings his hooked fingers to his mouth and lets a clear whistle rip. It cuts through the sunny afternoon and quiets the crowd.

Which is just what Elsa needs.

She raises her arms for more quiet, then motions everyone closer. They inch nearer to her—their guard up. That can't be missed. Well, Elsa can figure surprises don't often fare well with this bunch. Recent surprises seem to have been *bad* news more often than good. So she's glad to change that. Right now.

"Well, everyone," Elsa calls out. "It's really nice to be together casually like this today," she begins. "But—"

A few groans and a random *Oh, no* stop her and get her squinting at the impatient crowd until there's silence again.

"*But*," she finally goes on, "things aren't as casual as I'd like. Between everything—marriage issues, and near-accidents, and, well, fraught brother reunions, and ... and a dramatic vow renewal—" Again, she's stopped. This time it's by a late-summer bug circling her head. She swats it away. "That's what I mean. Just like that, things are getting out of control. I realize I'm no help, either. The inn's on and off again. Celia's been left unemployed in the process. Oh, there's been a *lot* of upheaval lately."

"But that's just life, Elsa," Kyle offers from his food trays.

"We can get through things," Lauren insists.

"As long as we're still all together," Paige adds, motioning to everyone gathered 'round.

"Right. But there's a nervous undercurrent here—I *feel* it. Things just aren't settled down this summer. So," Elsa says, holding up an open hand when Jason tries to interject. "So here's what we're doing. Tomorrow. Celia and I are hosting a *calm-down* luncheon at the Ocean Star Inn."

Celia steps forward then. "*Everyone's* invited," she continues for Elsa. "We'll have lunch. And ... and take a *breath*. Sit back. Relax and start the new week on the right foot." As she says it, she reaches around Aria still strapped to her and waggles the baby's sandaled foot.

"Bring your appetites, all. *Mangia, mangia!*" Elsa goes on.

"On the menu? Sandwiches on gourmet breads. Specialty side dishes, too."

That does it. Everyone erupts with high-fives and *whoops* and exclamations. Matt, Kyle, Jason, Cliff, Vinny—and the women, too.

Yes!
Elsa's Sunday meals are back!
Gotta get ourselves into trouble more often.
Hell, yeah. More trouble, more table time.
Well, it's ABOUT time.
Sweet. I dib ... everything!
Get in line behind me, punk.
Man, my mouth's watering already.

fourteen

SHANE MADE GOOD TIME.

He skipped Alex's tattoo, thanked Shiloh and his parents for hosting and booked it out of the barn brunch.

Stopped home and booked it straight here, too.

Pedal to the metal the whole way from Maine—straight to Stony Point. Nothing but highway pavement and divided lines blurred past as he hit the road with only an overnight duffel tossed in his pickup's front seat.

Finally, the stone train trestle's in front of him, and it's just after six o'clock.

Finally, he slows up. It feels like he's taking his first deep breath in nearly five hours. Okay, so if anything, it shows him just how much this place—or these people—mean to him.

~

Shane drives through the dark tunnel now and stops at the guard post, only to see Nick across the street at the guard shack. He's pressing large blue rectangles of sample paint colors onto the shingled walls.

Shane tips up his newsboy cap. "Yo, Nick," he calls out the window.

"Hey! You're back," Nick says.

"That I am."

"But you're definitely not supposed to be …"

"Right again."

"So, what's up?" Nick crosses the street to the truck. On his way, he throws a glance over his shoulder at the paint samples, then trots to Shane. "What'd you do, forget something? Had to make the trip back?"

Shane nods. *I forgot something, all right,* he thinks. *My whole damn life's here, it seems. And lately I don't want to leave it behind.* But he says none of that. "Forget something?" Shane repeats instead. "Yeah. Yeah, something like that."

"Well, hey. Stop in and see the Barlows while you're here. They have some shindig going on. Everyone's there."

"Really? Thought Maris had a close call. Heard she just missed a bad accident that shook the two of them up."

"She did." Nick leans a hand on Shane's open window. "And now they're celebrating life in that big old cottage on the bluff."

"*Ha.* That's decent. Maybe I'll head over later. We'll see," Shane says, putting his truck in gear and tipping his cap. When Nick backs up a few steps as the truck starts rolling, Shane points to the shabby guard shack stickered here and there with random blue squares. "Try some grays!" he yells before rounding the curve and driving the winding beach roads.

Now, with the thought of some life celebration going down at the Barlows', Shane wastes no time. Grabbing his duffel, he rushes into his rented bungalow. The air inside is dank and musty after being closed up for just two days. So he stops in the living room and shoves open the sticking paned windows there. Turning then, he can't miss the stalled checkers game just waiting for him and Celia.

"*Not right now*," he whispers, picking up his duffel and heading down the hallway. After splashing some water on his face in the bathroom, he changes into a dark khaki long-sleeve Henley, fresh jeans and scuffed-up boat shoes. Pushes back those shirtsleeves, adds his braided leather cuff, belts his jeans and runs a hand through his hair.

The whole day's been at him. Push, pull. Maine, Connecticut. Good times, worrying. Barn brunch, Kyle's phone call. Fast, slow. Accelerate on the highway, cruise under the trestle. Back, forth. This way, that. Go, stop.

Which Shane finally does.

He stops.

Stops and blows out a long breath.

Gets something to drink, too. In the kitchen, he fills a tall glass with cold water and takes it out onto the back porch. After hoisting himself up onto the half-wall, he just sits there and rolls out some kinks in his neck. Sips his water, too, as he takes in the distant sight of Long Island Sound. The sun will be setting soon so the water's steel gray in the low light. And still, too. Not a breeze ripples the sea.

Shane takes in that calm view. The drive here had been intense. His focus, tunnel vision. Because it felt important that he be here for Jason and Maris. Their situation

115

yesterday sounded serious. And if anyone knows one thing for certain, Shane does.

He knows what it's like to *not* have the comfort of old friends around. Fifteen years alone taught him that real well.

But he feels the five-hour drive now and rolls his neck again. Rests his hand on the back of it and tips up his head. No doubt Celia will be at the Barlows'. He's sure *everyone* will be there. That's a given. And how this place works. So it might be time to write Celia a note, actually. He can slip it to her if she's there.

Because Lord knows, something she said before their checkers game two nights ago has stayed with him. And, hell, he sure wouldn't mind knowing more, either. So before leaving for the Barlows', Shane grabs a notepad and pen and stops at the kitchen counter in his cottage. With his hand to the paper, he leans there. Taps his pen on the countertop. Thinks a moment, then scrawls a one-line letter to the woman he loves. His hand quickly moves across the pad before he signs the note, folds it in half, slips it into his pocket and heads out.

~

"You dressed up."

Maris turns from her mirror to see Jason in the doorway.

"Going somewhere?" he asks, stepping into the room.

"What?" While slipping on her silver medallion necklace, she looks down at her lightweight V-neck sweater and cropped patchwork-denim jeans. The jeans have overlapping denim swatches and random distressing and a frayed hem. "Jason! This is *not* dressed up. It's casual," she insists while half-tucking the black sweater.

"Okay." He crosses the room and kisses her then. "Casual and beautiful, too."

"And yes, I *am* going somewhere, actually," Maris says, turning to her dresser again, leaning close to the mirror and putting on silver stud earrings.

"Where?"

"Well, your lounging-in-bed idea was good. Really good—while it lasted. But it was interrupted all day with everyone's *good* intentions. And to be honest?" Maris goes on, turning toward Jason as he's straightening their messy bed now. "I was feeling a little stir-crazy up here. So Taylor helped me pick out a fun outfit before she left, and now I'm going downstairs."

"Believe me, sweetheart," Jason says as he drops onto the bed, "they're *exhausting* down there."

"But they're our friends!" Maris insists, tidying up her loose braid as she does.

Jason plumps a pillow behind him as he sits there. "Friends with whom we're apparently having Sunday lunch tomorrow."

"Tomorrow?"

"At Elsa's. It's a *calm-down* luncheon after all the chaos of this summer. She and Celia are hosting."

"That actually sounds really nice," Maris is saying as she swipes on lip gloss at the dresser mirror.

"I guess Elsa wants to do it for you and me, too. Bring back her Sunday meals. Which is fine by me," Jason adds while flipping his hourglass, then lying back on his fluffed pillow and closing his eyes.

"*Oh*, no. No, no, no, Mr. Barlow. You can't be dozing for an *hour*." In clip footsteps, Maris hurries to where he's trying to sleep. She also picks up the pillow beside him. "*Up*, mister."

Instead of getting up, Jason tosses an arm over his eyes. "Few minutes," he manages.

So ... she does it. Maris takes that pillow and swats it across his chest. "Up, hon," she says, laughing.

As if he'd let that go—being pillow-whacked. As if his hand isn't pulling the pillow from beneath his head. He takes that pillow and sits up, squinting at her as she cautiously steps back. But she's not quick enough to miss getting pillow-smacked right across her hip.

"*Ooh*, Jason." Maris spins back to him and reaches for her pillow on the bed. As she does, he grabs hold of her arm, then her waist and pulls her right down on the mattress with him. They're a tumble of arms and legs and pillows and sheets, then. And laughter—plenty of that. And pillow shoves, and ducks, and playful pillow hits and blocks.

"You'll mess my hair!" Maris breathlessly says. "And I just fixed up your braid."

"Really?" Instead of tossing another pillow her way, he reaches for that braid. "It looks nice tousled," Jason tells her, his voice dropping.

They quiet now. But are still breathing hard from the mini pillow fight. He toys with her braid. Maris leans on the headboard and touches his face.

"*Jason*," she whispers.

And quickly sits up when she hears someone in the doorway.

"Maris?" her sister asks. Eva stands there wearing a light

sweater topper over a tie-dyed T-shirt dress. "Kyle told me to bring you a plate of food," she's saying as she slowly walks into the room. She stops, though, and eyes the messed-up pillows and bedcovers, and the sand falling through the hourglass bulb, and Jason adjusting one of those wayward pillows, then crooking his arm beneath his head and flopping down on it. "*What* is going on?" Eva asks as she veers to Maris' side of the bed now.

Maris, instead of answering, just opens her arms to her sister. So Eva squeezes that plate of what looks like chicken wings onto the nightstand, leans over and gives Maris a good, old-fashioned hug. It's one that's all sighs and rocking back and forth.

"I thought the *worst* when you said you almost wrecked the car," Eva says into the hug. "Don't scare me like that *ever* again, okay?"

When she pulls back from that sister-hug, Maris extends a hand. "Pinkie swear," she says, before explaining somewhat about staying in bed all day to unwind. She glances at the pillows randomly tossed on the bed, then at Eva. "But things maybe got out of control," she adds with a wink.

Eva scoots closer to Maris on the mattress. "I feel like I maybe walked in on something here?"

"Little bit," Jason admits as he gets up. He leans over and kisses the top of Maris' head before crossing the bedroom to the door.

Maris blows him a kiss, then gets up, too, and starts straightening the bed. Eva helps her as they adjust the coverlet and neatly stack the pillows.

"So you're *really* fine?" Eva asks. "And not just saying you are so I won't worry?"

"Cross my heart," Maris assures her while fluffing a pillow. "The thing is, what happened last night made me feel pretty down."

"Aww, hon."

Maris nods. "Waking up today and realizing how quickly life can change?" she says with a snap of her fingers. "Like *that*? It made me sad ... and regretting my own choices this summer."

"You mean, with Jason?"

"Oh, yeah. And on top of it all? He walked in on me bawling like a baby. Real early this morning."

"Oh no—Maris!" Eva drops onto Jason's bedside chair.

"Yep." Maris slaps some wrinkles out of the coverlet now. "I thought he was outside doing yard work. Didn't even hear him come upstairs for a hat as I had a good cry."

"My God. What happened then?"

"Jason being incredible Jason ... well, he calmed me down." Maris sits on the edge of the mattress. "Suggested this whole day of lounging in bed and catching our breath."

"That's so sweet," Eva says from Jason's chair. "And I'm not surprised."

"Really?"

Eva pauses. "He loves you so much, Mare. I saw that firsthand when I went out to Sullivan's place about ... two weeks ago now. Labor Day evening. Dropped off a platter of chicken cutlets before my real estate conference. And let me tell you, I've *never* seen someone more worried."

"Me and Jason both, huh?" With a sigh, Maris falls back onto the neatened bed. "A couple of worrywarts."

Eva shrugs, then. "Take it or leave it. That's the Barlows for you. Come to think of it, that's the Gallaghers. The

DeLucas. The Bradfords. Hell, that's all of us—all worrywarts. And they're *all* outside on your deck."

"Good, because I'm famished," Maris tells her as she sits up and lifts that plate of chicken wings off her nightstand. "I'll have this outside with the gang."

Eva gets up from the chair. "Well the party's really cooking, sis. So let's go." She takes Maris by the arm and gives a tug in that direction.

Maris nods, but slows. Because there's one thing she just *can't* neglect. Can't forget to do. "Wait!" she tells Eva, depositing the dinner plate in her sister's hands. "Hold this for me?" she asks before turning to Jason's nightstand and picking up his pen and architectural journal. She opens it and whispers while jotting *Pillow fight, 15 minutes* in their lost-time log.

fifteen

EARLY THAT EVENING WHILE STILL at the Barlows', Elsa feels the sea damp pressing in. So she steals away to the driveway, where her golf cart is parked. The scarf she'd left tied there will feel good against that damp. But while wrapping the scarf around her neck, she stops. Stops with an idea that's been simmering all day.

"*Psst! Celia!*" Elsa sort of whisper-calls, giving the scarf a shake up toward the deck. "Come *here.*"

Celia squints down into twilight's shadows. Behind her on the deck, people hang out. They carry dishes of appetizers and walk around, sit at the patio table, have a laugh with Kyle at the hot plates. A few tiki torches are lit along the deck railings, too. "Elsa?" Celia calls back when she spots her.

"*Shh!*" Elsa aggressively waves her hand, beckoning her to the backyard.

And Celia goes. With Aria strapped to her chest in a baby sling, she carefully holds the railing and descends the stone steps off the deck. But the closer she gets to Elsa, the more Elsa backs up—deeper into the yard.

"*Okaaay,*" Celia says when she finally catches up. She takes Elsa's arm, but glances furtively back at the folks up on the deck before turning to Elsa. "You've got that look in your eye again."

"What look?" Elsa asks, loosely tying the silk scarf now.

"The one that says you're *up* to something. For the second time today!"

"Am I ever." Elsa pulls Celia into nearby shadows. In the dusky light, Aria's cooing and moving her arms toward Elsa; the big maple tree towers over them. It's good that the sun's setting, too—they blend right in with the early darkness. Elsa glances to the house, where those tiki torches flicker on wavering silhouettes of the others. Confident that she and Celia are safe from prying eyes, she finally leans close to her. "Since we're back in good graces, I have to ask you something *really* important."

"Oh, no. What now?"

"This." Elsa gives *another* quick glance to the crowded deck, then winks at Celia. "Want to get into some trouble with me?"

"*What?*"

"You heard me."

"What's gotten into you? *Trouble? Are you serious?*"

"Never more so."

"Huh. I could be game for some good troublemaking. What do you have in mind now, foxy lady?"

Elsa pulls Celia closer and relays her antics. She glosses over the details, adds a little intrigue, then steps back to gauge Celia's response.

Well. Celia straightens, squints through the evening light at Elsa and holds her gaze for a long moment. "*Wait here,*" Celia whispers. She hurries to the bottom of the deck stairs, where Aria's stroller is parked on the grass.

All the while, Elsa stays hidden in the backyard and watches Celia discreetly wheel that stroller her way. She's slinking through a fringe of shadows so that no one much notices her. No one sees her devious stroller-maneuverings around a golf cart, past Maddy's wading pool, beside the tall maple tree. Finally, Celia stops near Elsa and points the stroller in the direction of the old barn there. She shifts Aria still in her sling, too, before turning to Elsa.

"Ready?" Elsa asks.

Celia gives a single nod. "Let's do this."

"*You sure?*" Elsa whispers.

"Oh, yes," Celia says as they join forces in the twilight. "I'm in."

~

Their talk is hushed.

It's stealthy, even—there's no missing that—not with the way Elsa and Celia lean close and murmur as they slip in through Jason's barn-studio door. Inside, they stop and freeze. Their heads are tipped; Elsa has a finger to her lips. There are voices talking outside, and dishes clattering up on the deck. They listen a bit more. When they're certain no one notices their absence, Celia makes the first move. She lifts Aria out of the sling looped around her shoulders and settles the baby in the stroller now. Celia's actions are silent and smooth. Her auburn hair falls forward as she straps the baby in. After wheeling Aria aside, Celia reaches to a clip-on toy bar and gives a fuzzy animal a rattle. "*Look, Aria!*" she whispers, bending low. "*A spotted giraffe.*" She touches Aria's hand to the dangling toy.

When the baby gurgles and coos, Celia turns to Elsa and slowly pushes the stroller across the wide-planked wood floor. They stop right at the bottom of the stairs to the loft.

And freeze again.

And look up at the mounted moose head.

"How are we going to pull this off?" Celia asks. Standing there in her striped tee and skinny jeans, she gives the stroller one more waggle, then puts her hands on her hips and squints up at that moose.

"Give me a sec. We'll figure something out." Elsa eyes the moose, too. She steps from one side of the staircase to the other, all while scrutinizing the animal mounted on the wall at the top of the stairs.

The barn studio is quiet for these few moments. Only the hum of voices from the deck reaches them. There's the late-summer katydids' scratchy chirp starting up outside, too. Flickering tiki lights framing the deck can be seen through the barn's double slider.

Inside the barn, though, there's little light. Wall-mounted brass accent lamps glimmer over Jason's massive framed cottage-renovation photographs. And Celia *had* turned on some of the recessed ceiling lighting, setting it to dim. So there's just enough soft, vague illumination to plot their moves.

"You know, Elsa ..." Celia admits. "Sneaking in here like this, I kind of get a funny feeling."

"Like what?" Elsa asks.

"Like Jason Barlow would *kill* us if he ever caught us in here—*stealing*. Because, yes," Celia adds, motioning to the moose head, "this *is* stealing. And I'm not really sure about it."

"No. No. Let me explain, Cee. The story of the moose head is that it's *always* been stolen. *But*," Elsa's harsh whisper insists now, "*it's rightfully mine!*"

"Yours?"

Elsa nods. "Because it was stolen from Foley's! It was originally hanging there all those years ago. But someone stole it and put it *here*—in the Barlow barn. Even before it was Jason's architect studio. So, you know ... Jason gets the original Foley's jukebox *and* the original moose head? How fair is that?" Elsa climbs the first step to the loft and gets nearer to that moose. After another few steps, she stretches around and tries to examine how the moose's head is attached to the wall. With a shrug of her shoulders then, she walks down the stairs and returns to Celia's side. "I want that moose head back and hanging prominently—for our calm-down luncheon tomorrow."

"*What?* By *tomorrow?*"

"Damn it, yes." Elsa crosses her arms and drops her voice. "Because let me tell you something. During the inn's reno, Jason *made* me leave the spot open on the wall where that thing was mounted."

"You mean in the back room? That ... that empty gold frame hanging there?"

"You got it. Just like in the museums when a painting is stolen. You know how the museums leave an empty frame where the painting *should* be to signify the theft?" Elsa grabs Celia's arm then and pulls her into the shadows. "*Wait, Cee.*

126

Did you hear something just now?"

"Don't move. *Shh.*" Celia puts a finger to her pursed lips and turns to check on Aria in the stroller. The baby's eyes are closed, her head tipped as she dozes there now. Still, the two women stand motionless. "Okay," Celia says seconds later. "Must've been a noise from out on the deck. Now let's get this done, *quick.*" She moves close to the stairs, stopping only to tell Elsa, "Keep an eye out for me. I'm going up." Gingerly then, Celia tiptoes up each step until she's within touching distance of that moose head. She reaches a hand to it and strokes its neck. Her fingers skim its long, fuzzy muzzle next, right down between its wide-set nostrils. "How will we *ever* get you down?" she asks while gazing into the moose's glass eyes. She looks over her shoulder at Elsa. "Would a ladder help?"

"Shoot, it's out in the side yard. Cliff was using it."

"For *what?*"

"He was trimming the hedges for Jason."

"Are you kidding me?" Celia takes a sharp breath and leans against the stair railing. But she doesn't stop eyeing that moose head. "Oh my God. We're going to get caught. We're *so* going to get caught! Busted. Hauled out of here. You pick the worst-case scenario—we're in for it."

"No. No, we're not," Elsa sternly says. "Just *focus.*"

"Okay." Celia blows out a breath. "*Focusing* ... Okay, so the ladder's out. But if we even manage to get this thing off the wall, then what?"

Elsa looks from the dozing baby to Celia. "Put it in my golf cart."

"But everyone will see it!"

Elsa walks up a few steps—high enough to just touch

that moose's nose. "We can put a garbage bag over it maybe," she suggests, studying the wide antlers atop the moose's head.

"I don't know." There's a change in Celia's voice. Defeat is creeping in. Her words go a little monotone. "It's getting late. And any minute now, people will miss us outside. Plus, that thing just looks *too* heavy, Elsa."

"It *is* a lot bigger up close than I thought it would be. "

"Well, if we think fast. Let's see. Maybe Jason has something here we can dismount it with." Celia turns on the stairs to scan his studio for some tool. Or some *apparatus* that might help. She stands there and slowly looks around the deeply shadowed space.

And *gasps*. "*Shane!*" Celia loudly whispers.

Elsa spins around, too, and freezes right there with Celia on the loft stairs. Both of them squint across the room—straight at him.

Straight to where he's leaning on the shadowed wall right beside the slider. Celia and Elsa's steady gaze through the shadows gets him to shift his position now. He'd walked to the Barlows' from his cottage. Interesting detour happened, though, when he noticed these two sneaking around near the barn as he headed up Jason's long driveway. So he followed behind them—and hasn't moved from his wall spot ever since sneaking in the screen slider just like they did. In fact, he's been watching their every move—with some amusement, too.

Now Shane crosses his arms and eyes them both while asking one question. "You ladies need some help?"

sixteen

SHIT, I CAN'T *BELIEVE* YOU'RE here," Kyle says
when he walks through the barn studio's double slider later.
Shane's checking out that moose head at the top of the loft
stairs. "I just called you a few hours ago!" Kyle goes on
while maneuvering in an aluminum stepladder, then closing
the slider behind him. "Don't you have to get on a lobster
boat?"

"First thing Monday morning."

"And you came all this way *here*? Today?"

"I did. For the Barlows."

"Crazy, man." Kyle sets the ladder beside the stairs and
veers over to Jason's drafting table. He pulls out the
wheeled stool and sits himself down for a minute.

"Anyone see you head to the barn?" Shane asks.

"No, I don't think so." Kyle glances back at the double
slider. "How about you? Anyone notice you? Besides Celia
and Elsa?"

"Just Nick at the trestle," Shane tells him as he reaches for that moose head and gives it a little test shove. "And leave it to those two ladies, huh?" He looks over his shoulder at Kyle. "I see they got you over here without a hitch."

"Sure did. Elsa pulled me aside on the deck and told me something was wrong with her golf cart. Asked me to check it out. I was *clueless* until she got me away from my serving station—*and* any people within earshot. She steered me here then with a real quick explanation." Kyle gives the stool a slow spin and takes in the sight of Jason's studio. Beneath the low illumination of a few recessed lights, he makes out some details: the wall shelves lined with leather and canvas journals; a massive L-shaped office desk around the corner; tubes of blueprints; Maris' old denim loft upstairs; moonlight shining in through her stained-glass wave window.

"Yo," Shane calls from the stairs. "You ever getting off that stool?"

"Yeah, I'm coming." Kyle gets up and walks to the stairs now. "So. We're *really* stealing this moose?"

"You up to it, bro?" Shane asks, trying to somewhat jimmy up that mounted head.

"Hell, yeah. It's not the first time I lifted that thing." Kyle fists his hands, then opens them wide as he extends his arms and does some stretching. "Have a feeling it won't be the last time, either."

The moose shifts a little when Shane reaches beneath it and manages to press it upward. "What do you think it weighs?"

"Seventy pounds, maybe? Eighty?" Kyle scrutinizes the

moose head from where he stands. "It's a doozy. Could be a four-foot spread on the antlers?"

"Pretty damn close, anyway." Shane pushes up the sleeves of his Henley shirt. "Got our work cut out for us. So let's *go*—before Jason catches us, man."

"It'd be our heads on the wall, then."

"No shit." Shane glances over to the double slider. "So move it. *Move* it. Got to be *fast* while Elsa and Celia distract everyone on the deck."

"On it," Kyle says, opening the ladder now at the base of the stairs and setting it as close to that moose head as possible.

"Where'd you grab the ladder? Elsa said Cliff was cutting hedges with it earlier."

"He was. But Jason moved it back to his shed. It was leaning up against the outside wall like it was just waiting for me."

Shane glances toward the slider again. "Think Barlow will suspect us?"

"Not if we do this right. He'll be plenty shocked, though." Kyle climbs that ladder then. His feet clump on each rung until he gets to the top step. "You tell Elsa to leave the inn's deck door unlocked? You know, to get inside the back room?"

"Nah," Shane answers from where he's standing on the stairs. "She gave me the key."

"Sweet." Kyle reaches to the moose from the ladder. "Hey, dude. Those antlers are detachable, you know. Would it be easier if we take them off?"

"No. No time tonight. Got to get the *hell* outta here. *Quick*." From his perch on the stairs, Shane looks over at Kyle. "Come on," Shane says. "Let's get this done. *Now!*"

And in the shadows, they both reach for the mounted moose head.

⌒

Oddly, Kyle feels safer after they thank God for Jason's double-door slider. Because they *easily* get that moose head—antlers and all—through it and outside into the darkness. Heck, they actually might have a fighting chance of pulling this stunt off. He and Shane both carry that large moose head down the few barn steps before veering behind Jason's shed. What happens next is a blur of whispered words, and running, and hiding, and swearing, and catching their breath. And sweating; Lord, do they sweat.

Is the coast clear?

Good. Go!

Footsteps, then. Footsteps and heavy breathing as they lug that moose head across the dark lawn behind the Barlow house.

Shit, headlights! Someone's pulling up in the driveway!

Fuck. Where do I go?

Panicked looks around, then more whispered orders as the moose weighs them down.

There! Get behind the hedges!

A break now. The moose is set on the grass. They shake out their arms. Breathe. Look around. Wipe their faces. As they wait out the car parking with its intrusive headlights, they stay hidden and listen to the other part of this plot playing out on the ladies' side. It's all happening up on the deck as Celia and Elsa distract everyone from the bona fide theft going down.

Celia to Jason: *Would you mind if I use that new stove of yours?*

Jason's answer: *Not at all. You cooking something?*

Celia again: *Have to heat up Aria's bottle. She's really hungry. But can you possibly show me how to turn on those fancy burners? By the way, the new kitchen is gorgeous!*

"That gets Jason out of the picture," Shane says when he stretches around and sees Jason and Celia go inside.

"Think Aria's really ready for a bottle?"

"Don't know. Could be a ruse."

"Shit. Corrupting that sweet baby at such a young age."

Elsa then: *Who wants seconds?*

And Vinny with his plate: *Load 'er up, Elsa.*

Nick, too: *Make room, Vincenzo.*

Lauren and Maris, next: *Ahem. Ladies first, boys?*

Elsa again, dawdling this time: *Let me adjust the flame. Don't want to burn anything. And choose carefully, there's only so much to go around.*

"Oh, she's good," Shane says. "They'll be deliberating that food for ten minutes. So let's go."

"*Ready?*" Kyle whispers.

Shane nods. "On three." They both bend and get a firm grip of the moose head. "One. Two. And … *three.*"

"*Quick, quick!*" Kyle utters as they round the bend to the front of the Barlow house.

A quick *stop* then, too. They bend low and squint into the moonlit night to confirm the coast is clear. It is. So their feet thud across the dewy lawn.

"Careful now," Kyle tells Shane as they take calculated steps down the sloping lawn toward the street. That heavy full moon throws enough light to see that no one's around. "Let's get out while the gettin's good."

Shane walks backward as they swing around to position the moose head in Kyle's pickup truck bed. When Kyle grabs an old blanket from the backseat, Shane balances the moose on the tailgate. Finally, Kyle spreads the blanket across the truck bed before again hefting his side of eighty pounds of moose. There are a few grunts, then. A few choice cuss words as they lift together in the evening's dark shadows. Next, they maneuver and shift and duck—this time on the other side of the truck—when a couple happens by on a nighttime walk. But finally the moose head is settled atop that blanket in the back of Kyle's truck.

"*Hurry up. Hurry up*," Kyle warns when Shane climbs in the truck bed to carefully secure the merchandise in place.

Shane works his way around the moose and adjusts it here, there. "Shit, this thing's a beast."

There's some thudding around in the truck. They both duck again when a car drives past on the street. But a minute later, Shane's jumping out of the truck bed and closing the tailgate.

"Good to go?" Kyle asks from where he's waiting at the curb.

"Yep. Give me your keys," Shane tells him.

"*What?*" Kyle lifts his black tee and dabs the perspiration on his face. "*You're* not driving my new wheels."

"Listen, bro. You can't come. You'll be missed if you're gone any longer. Someone will be onto you and the moose jig will be up. But no one even knows *I'm* here, so makes *no*

134

difference if I'm gone," Shane says, snapping his fingers for the truck keys. "And don't worry. I'll be *right* back."

"Damn it. You go easy on my new vehicle, or I'll cream you," Kyle tells him when he tosses the keys his way. "But wait. You can't haul that thing up Elsa's deck stairs yourself," Kyle says, walking closer as Shane climbs in the pickup's driver's seat.

"Oh, shit. You're right. So ... how about this? I'll slide it out right on that blanket and put it beneath the deck. Elsa said she keeps some yard quilts there. You give Elsa her key back, and I can wrap up the moose nice and snug at her place. We'll hang it first thing in the morning."

"Okay." Kyle squints through the shadows when raucous laughter sounds from the Barlow deck out back. "But *early*, man," Kyle insists, turning to Shane with a pointed finger. "The Sunday crowd at the diner is a sight to behold. I *can't* be late to work."

"No prob." Shane starts the truck engine.

"And remember. *No* funny stuff with my truck," Kyle warns as he backs away from the curb. "Don't touch the mirrors, seat, controls, radio. Nothing. I got it all set just how I want it."

"Don't *worry*."

But yep, Kyle thinks, *he's doing it anyway*. Shane's adjusting the rearview mirror before looking out at the Barlow house all illuminated in the night.

"I'll be back here in fifteen or so," Shane's saying. "Park this baby *right* here. No one will even notice your truck was gone. And I'll treat it mighty fine," he says, gently patting the dashboard as he does.

Like hell.

Because the first thing Shane does after putting the truck in gear is this: He chirps the hefty tires and smokes them up—just a little—as he careens down the sandy beach road.

"*You bastard*," Kyle says under his breath. Shakes his fist at the departing truck, too, before laughing and turning away in the night.

seventeen

HE DID IT.

Shane backed Kyle's new truck right up to the storage entrance beneath Elsa's upper-level deck. He also found an old wooden table under that deck. The dusty table was covered with random clay pots and an extra garden hose—which Shane quickly set on the ground. That done, he dragged the table to the entrance and lined it up with the truck's open tailgate. Everything after that was a piece of cake. A few good shoves, a little twisting and turning—and that moose head slid from the truck bed to its nighttime home atop that big wooden table.

Still in the under-the-deck storage area, Shane uses the flashlight on his cell phone now. In its beam, he finds Elsa's plastic tote stuffed with folded yard quilts. Lo and behold, he manages to drop some over that moose head—antlers and all. As he's finagling a second quilt over those antlers, his cell phone dings with a text message.

"*In a minute,*" Shane whispers, his arms reaching across that four-foot antler span.

Stepping back then, he squints into the shadows beneath the deck. A few Adirondack chairs are stacked there. A wrought-iron bistro table. A birdbath. And no one would know the difference. No one would know that the evidence—a stuffed moose head—is right here, too. Practically hidden in plain sight.

"Good to go," Shane tells himself, closing the pickup's tailgate and hopping in the truck. But before he takes off for the Barlows', he checks that waiting text on his phone.

"*Ah, Celia,*" he whispers, seeing her message in the dark truck cab. *If you can steal away,* he reads, *I'm walking Aria home. Will be on road near marsh for next 10 mins.*

⌒⌒

The marsh is a different world at night. It gets the attention of every physical sense. Small splashes in the salty water are eerily heard, but unseen. The chorus of insects—of chirps and whistles—comes steady beneath moonlight. Misty salt air rises. That air's touch is damp. Whispering marsh grasses become whispering shadows.

Which is all good. He and Celia blend right in with those shadows as he keeps slow pace with her. She's pushing Aria's stroller along the beach road while he barely coasts in Kyle's truck beside them.

"Did you get the moose there okay?" Celia right away asks him.

"Sure did."

"*Phew!* And Elsa was leaving in her golf cart, right before

138

I took off," Celia tells him. "Did you see her there?"

Shane glances to his rearview mirror. "Must've just missed her. Hightailed it out of her place as soon as I got that moose head delivered. Be hanging it first thing tomorrow."

"I know. Kyle told me and Elsa back at the Barlows'."

"Yep. And I have to say, I'm kind of surprised you two pulled this thing off."

"With some help." Celia gets a sly smile. "But Elsa had her heart set on it. And really wanted me in on it, too. So I figured it's all in good fun, you know?"

"Tell that to Barlow when he realizes that moose head is missing."

"Yeah." While wheeling Aria along, Celia squints over at Shane in the driver's seat. Manages to slap his arm hooked on the open window, too. "Speaking of which, when I saw you standing in Jason's barn studio? I just about jumped out of my *skin*."

"Couldn't miss that, and the way you stifled your reaction."

"I mean, are you crazy? What are you *doing* here again?"

Shane nudges up his newsboy cap and glances to the saltwater marsh. The heavy full moon hangs low over it. "Finding any reason in the book to stay."

"But you have to be careful," Celia tells him, still stroller-wheeling. "With all that driving back and forth, you'll be tired. For work."

Shane only shrugs. "Can I see you later? At your place?"

"After you visit Jason and Maris?"

"Yeah."

Celia gives a slow nod. "You *know* I'd like that." For a second, there's only the sound of the stroller wheels turning over the sand-coated road. "You can use the beach path to get there. No one will even notice."

"Okay." Shane stops the truck and motions Celia closer. When she steps to the window, he leans out and steals a quick kiss. Does something else, too. Reaches for the letter folded into his shirt pocket. "Thought I'd deliver this one in person," he says, handing her the note. When she takes it, he gradually veers the truck to a side street—in the direction of the Barlows'. "Read it and you can answer me later," he quietly calls back, giving a wave as he takes off.

eighteen

ARIS," EVA SAYS LATER THAT evening. "This kitchen! I mean ... *wow!*"

Maris nods while lifting a barbecued chicken wing from her plate. She and her sister sit side by side at her new kitchen island. The two crystal pendant chandeliers glimmer above. Damp sea air drifts in through the slider screen, the open windows. "Thanks," she manages around a mouthful of food. "Jason and I are really enjoying it."

"I can see why. Because this?" Eva goes on as she slips out of her sweater topper and drapes it over her stool back. "This is what kitchens are for. Eating. Hanging out." She finishes the last of her cheeseburger slider. "Everything happens in the kitchen, don't you think?"

"Apparently the *outdoor* kitchen, too." Maris hitches her head to the deck. "Would you just look at that?"

"At what?"

"The guys." Kyle, Matt and Jason pass by just outside

the slider. They're headed down the deck stairs on some man-mission. The others are milling around with plates in hand, passing the flickering tiki torches, grabbing something off Kyle's hot plates. Voices rise and fall. Laughs come and go. "They won't leave."

Eva leans back for a better look. "They do seem pretty settled in."

"It's like they have their own *galaxy* out there." Maris stands and takes Eva's arm. "The way they just orbit the *whole* property." She tugs her sister up. "Come here."

"What?" Eva grabs a quick sip from a glass of wine before tagging along after Maris.

"Look at them," Maris is insisting. She's stopped at a living room window and peering out to the side yard.

Eva joins her and presses back a sheer curtain. "Who is *that?*" she asks, squinting into the evening's shadows.

"Nick. He's back—and off duty now," Maris tells her— right as Nick whips some Frisbee he found to Maddy. "And check this out." Maris tugs Eva to another window, one looking out past the front porch. She and her sister stand still and watch through the screen. Nick joins up with Vinny and Matt approaching there now. They're just silhouettes beneath the moonlight in the front yard. Vinny and Matt are holding a beer. They're motioning up to a peak over the porch, too. It's hard to decipher who's saying what, but the gist of their talk comes through.

Some type of house plaque would look sweet up there, no?
Yeah, yeah. I mean, the place is kind of like a compound.
I saw one on another cottage. The plaque was a black metal crab, with an initial between the claws.

I can picture something like that to really claim this as the Barlow place.

An emblem of some sort. A coastal emblem with the initial B on it.

Maris looks at Eva beside her. "An *emblem*?"

"Well," Eva says. "It kind of *is* a good idea."

"Oh, sure. And now this!" Maris tells her sister then, moving to the other front window. "Let's see what's happening here." She points to Jason in the night's shadows. He's looking at the now nicely-cut hedges with Cliff. Jason turns and motions to some long-wilted tiger lilies and tired black-eyed Susans bordering the porch, too. "*Listen*," Maris whispers, leaning to the screen.

"My son, Denny? He's a landscape architect," Cliff's saying as he looks the shrubs up and down. "He could give you some ideas to freshen things up."

"I mean … *plaques*? And new *landscaping*?" Maris asks Eva. "I'm happy with just my new kitchen!"

"Don't worry. They're just bullshitting." Eva leans low and glances outside to the shadows. "It's what they *love* to do."

And at the mention of Kyle maybe grilling potato chips somewhere, and someone saying they raided Eva's platter of deviled eggs, the guys are on the move again.

So are Eva and Maris. They circle around the house via all the windows and watch until a few minutes later, the *guys* have circled around the dark yard to the Barlow deck. They climb the stairs and settle in with plates of food left behind, and another beer or two.

"*See?*" Maris whispers to her sister as they huddle at the

kitchen slider now. "They orbited their *galaxy* and are back."

Kyle shows up a few minutes after the others. While climbing the stairs, he looks over his shoulder out into the night. "Yo, Barlow," he says to Jason leaning against a deck railing now. "You know you have a staircase going down the bluff?"

"Sure do."

"Shit, I took a walk to your old man's bench and sat there a minute." Kyle stands beside Jason but faces that distant bluff. With his hands pressed to the railing, Kyle goes on. "The way the moon was shining, the railing on those hidden stairs caught my eye. So I took a better look. Man, it's a rickety old thing."

"Yep." Jason turns around to face the bluff, too. "Been out of commission for years—those stairs. Seriously neglected and really dangerous to go down."

"What?" Nick walks over holding a cold beer. "Something's down there?"

"A staircase," Kyle tells him. "Barely. It's practically falling apart."

"Where's it go?" Nick asks, looking toward the sea now.

"To a nice stretch of sand—when the tide's out." Jason's facing that bluff still. Silver moonlight falls on Long Island Sound beyond. The ripples of the seawater glimmer beneath that big full moon.

"Sounds sweet, man," Nick tells him. "Got your own private beach?"

Jason turns away and leans on the deck railing again. "Only if you can get to it," he says, lifting a can of beer off that railing. "Which, in the stairs' current condition, you can't."

Kyle slaps Jason's shoulder on his way across the deck to the gas grill. "Put those stairs on your to-do list, Barlow," he advises. "Meanwhile, I'm going to grill us up more sliced potatoes. Five minutes a side, back in a flash."

"*You never told me that*," Eva hisses at her sister where they've been eavesdropping just inside the slider.

"Told you what?"

Eva gives Maris a little shove, too. "You have a stairway to the *sea* here?"

"I guess. I've only seen glimpses of it from the bluff. The stairs are completely overgrown with brush. And these wild dune grasses. It's *impossible* to get through."

With a long sigh, Eva gazes out past the deck toward the water. "Sounds *magical*, though," she murmurs, then heads to a stool at the kitchen island.

"It's not. Jason meant it when he said it's treacherous." Still at the slider screen, Maris squints out at the misty sea view in the distance. "The rope railings are frayed. Jason says the steps' boards are all seaworn and rotten." Someone crossing the driveway now gets Maris' attention and she pauses. She looks from the person approaching, to her sister sipping wine at the island. "Wait, Eva. Is that *Shane* coming up to the deck?" She motions Eva over. "No way! He's *here*?"

"Get out!" Eva brings her wineglass to the slider. "I guess he is. Thought he went back to Maine."

"Oh my God. This is ridiculous," Maris says. She squints out at Shane crossing the backyard. He's got on a simple Henley and jeans and his newsboy cap, too, as he nears the deck stairs.

"*What's* ridiculous?" Eva presses her.

"That." Maris nods to the men on the deck. "Because, really. The ladies left already. Lauren. Celia and the baby. Elsa. Even Paige."

"Are you sure about Paige?" Eva motions her wineglass to the right. "Because Vinny's over there."

"Yep. I'm sure. She wanted to get home to her kids and let the babysitter off the hook. So Jason told me Kyle's giving Vinny a ride home in his new truck later. And now *Shane* showed up?" Maris turns and sits at the island. She pours a splash of wine into her glass there. As she does, she's still talking. "So we've got ... what—" She pauses and counts on her fingers. "Okay, *seven* guys just hanging out here. And let's face it, they're *not* here to see me. I mean, it's not like I got *hurt* yesterday and they're all staying out of concern." She pauses to sip her wine. "My car didn't even get a scratch. Jason and I were just shaken up by it last night."

"Aw, hon. But everybody *does* care about you." As she says it, Eva looks out to the deck at the men—who are erupting in laughter. All of them.

So Maris simply raises an eyebrow at her.

"Well, sis." Eva looks from her, to the view outside.

And Maris knows that view—past the deck. She knows the lure of the enchanted moon rising over the bluff at night. The stars above ... and the ocean stars sparkling in moonlight below. The sea, the night sea.

Eva's voice grows wistful then. "I guess the guys will use *any* excuse to hang out with Jason. I mean, look what comes with it," she says, taking in that misty moonlit sight, too.

146

nineteen

A MYTHIC STAIRWAY TO THE sea.

Now that sounds pretty incredible. Shane hears the guys talking about it as he climbs the stone steps of the Barlow deck. So he nudges up his newsboy cap and glances toward that elusive staircase. A heavy full moon hangs over the distant bluff. There's a silhouette of some bench atop it. Shadowy patches of wild dune grasses, too. Beyond, the dark sea pulses beneath that misty silver moonlight. Shane could just imagine some rickety stairs winding down that steep rocky embankment.

But he doesn't picture it for long.

Not when something—*suddenly*—pelts him square in the chest.

"What the hell?" he utters as he grabs at what hit him.

"Hey. Shane," Cliff Raines calls from the top of the deck stairs. "You're here. Good. Now you can have that *blessed* domino back."

Shane looks from the domino in his hand, then back up to Cliff—right as the guys crowd behind him. But it's Kyle who sends down a greeting.

"Yo, bro!" he calls to Shane. "What a *surprise*. Nick said he saw you arrive at the trestle, but I didn't believe the punk."

"Why not?" Shane tosses back as he climbs the stairs.

"Never thought you'd get your ass here when I called you this morning."

When Shane reaches the deck, Kyle hooks him in a bro-hug and slaps his back.

"*Shit, you're smooth, man,*" Shane discreetly says into that slapping hug. Because it's all a ruse, that greeting. Kyle's acting like this is the first he's seen of him to cover the whole moose-head escapade.

And so it begins. The, *Good to see you again.* And, *How're you doing, man? Nick said you forgot something and had to come back.* And, *What's up? You just get here?* There are shoulder slaps, and someone asks, *Thought you were in Maine already. What's that, a ten-hour trip?*

"It is, there and back. After Kyle called and filled me in, I knew I wanted to see the Barlows with my own eyes." Shane shoves his newsboy cap in his back pocket. "Dropped everything and here I am," he says, turning to Jason standing there in some black cargo shorts, a ratty Yale tee and work boots. Shane reaches out and shakes his hand.

"Unbelievable, man," Jason tells him. "That means a lot."

"Least I could do. Hey, where's your wife, guy? Heard she had a close call."

Jason nods to the kitchen door. "Inside with her sister."

148

"Okay. Hang on here." Shane slaps Jason's arm and walks past him to the slider. "And don't say anything important till I'm back," he warns over his shoulder.

⌒⌣

It's more of the same inside the impressive, renovated Barlow kitchen.

Once Maris and Eva see him, it's more smiles and hugs and shocked surprise beneath glimmering recessed lights. Beside stonework around the stove alcove. Near new state-of-the-art stainless-steel appliances.

Yep, it's more greetings.

And questions.

As Maris is in and out of cabinets for napkins and cups, the questions are from Eva. And with a different tone now; Shane doesn't miss that. Eva—ever protective of her long-lost sister—gives him the third degree. Hell, Shane feels like he's being interrogated in the local precinct as he tells her in *extended* detail why he made the trip.

"But weren't you ready to get back to work?" Eva asks, sitting at the kitchen island. "Heading out on the boat?"

"That's Monday." Arms crossed, Shane leans against a counter. "This morning, I was at a barn brunch for the lobster crew."

"Well if you were in Maine, how'd you even know a deer jumped in front of Maris' car?"

"Got the news from Kyle. He called during the brunch."

"And just like that, you're here?"

"No. Not just like *that*. Been a long, long day, Eva. Bailed on the brunch, packed a duffel with a change of clothes and *hightailed* it here."

"But ... couldn't you just have called?"

"Didn't feel right. You know, not giving moral support in *person* to my old friends."

"Eva!" Maris says while grabbing something from the fridge. "That's enough."

No more questions from Eva then. Just her squinting expression behind those sideswept bangs. So Shane answers even that doubting look. "Listen, Eva. These people here mean *everything* to me now."

"*Now?*" Eva asks, tipping her head.

Shane pauses. "Now that you're all back in my life ... thanks to Lauren reaching out to me this summer."

Which is enough for Sheriff Eva, apparently. She gets up off her stool and gives him a hug, then escorts him to his own stool. At the same time, Maris sets down a can of beer for him.

So Shane sits at the stunning new denim-blue island in the Barlow kitchen. Crystal pendant chandeliers hang above it. He also sees two wineglasses the sisters were working on. And the plates of food they'd pushed aside when he walked in. He turns to Maris as she's sliding over a bowl of freshly grilled-and-sea-salted potato chips.

"Listen, Mare," he tells her, glancing to the guys huddled outside. "I'm *really* glad you're okay. Seriously. Man, everyone had a good scare thinking of what you went through." He stands then. "But—"

With a wry smile, Maris holds up a hand and interrupts him. "I know. Don't tell me. You're headed out to the galaxy."

"The *what?*" Shane asks, picking up his beer and bowl of chips.

"Never mind." Maris opens the slider screen and motions him through—giving him a handful of extra napkins and cups to bring out for the other guys. "But it means a lot that you made the trip, Shane," she adds as he tucks the cups under his arm, balances the napkins atop his bowl and finagles his refreshments outside.

twenty

ON THE DECK, SCATTERED TIKI torches flicker in the night. Two or three lanterns burn, too—some on the patio table, one near the stone stairs. The nearby maple tree towers above, its leafy branches a dark shadow against the night sky.

"All right, fellas," Shane announces to the guys—some sitting around, some leaning on the deck railing. Shane sets his food and drink and cups and napkins on the table. "Got a hothead to deal with first." Crossing the deck then, Shane approaches Cliff at the far railing and takes him by the collar of a pocket crewneck tee he wears loose over gray jeans. "Now. What's your problem, Commish? Flinging your domino at me like that."

"You *stole* that domino once, and you know something, buster? You can have it back. It's *all* yours." Cliff gives Shane a shove and straightens his messed tee now. "That talisman's done me no favors."

Shane stands there and pulls the scuffed domino from his own shirt pocket. Flipping it in his hand, he eyes Cliff. "Why'd you need a favor from luck, Raines?"

"Doesn't matter now."

"Apparently it does," Shane answers, still flipping that domino. "Or else this thing wouldn't have hit, *bull's-eye*, on my chest."

Funny how all around them, there's silence. Shane can't miss it. There are only heads turning this way, to him—and that way, to Cliff.

Until Kyle starts up from where he stands at his serving station. "Hell, just spill it already, Judge."

Cliff only glares at Kyle through the night's shadows.

"Yeah, come on, Cliff," Matt adds. "Nothing to be ashamed of."

"What?" Nick asks from the patio table. "Did I miss something here?"

"Cliff," Jason says, leaning against a railing. Turns up his hands at him, too.

"*Fine.*" Cliff crosses his arms over his chest. "Sorry about the domino, Shane. But you took a fancy to it once, so you can keep it. Especially after it did *nothing* to save my derailed marriage proposal to Elsa."

"*What?*" Nick stands so quickly, his chair nearly tips back. "Marriage proposal? How? *When?*"

"Wait. There's going to be a wedding?" Vinny asks while leaning to the table and scooping up a handful of those grilled potato chips.

"Not mine. Okay, fellas? Not anytime soon, anyway," Cliff admits, then grabs a beer can from a cooler and sits on a deck chair.

"You and Elsa?" Shane asks, dragging over another chair and sitting near Cliff. "You two were already like an old married couple the first time I saw you last month." Shane leans forward, elbows on his knees. "So ... what happened?"

Cliff hitches his head toward Kyle. "Your brother happened."

"Oh, mercy. Not again." Kyle's standing there in his wrinkled day-old chef clothes: black tee over black pants. Leaning against a deck railing now, he tips his head up to the sky, then looks at Cliff. "I thought we were over this."

Shane looks to Kyle. "How the hell'd *you* stop his proposal?"

Kyle picks up his beer can from the railing and takes a long swig. Presses the cold can to his forehead, too. "Took Lauren out for date night, that's how. Went to a sweet concert at the bandshell. Had a nice picnic basket, bottle of wine and ... well, okay. How was I to know the judge was gonna pop the question to Elsa? Me and Lauren set up our blanket beside them, totally clueless. So sue me, Cliff."

Cliff sort of sinks lower in his chair. Clasps his hands over his lap. "You and Lauren settling there? It was the end of my hopes and dreams ... is all I can say."

"*Whoa*, Cliff." Jason walks over and cuffs his shoulder. "You're in surrender mode. Not good, man."

"Yeah, boss. That'll get you nowhere—and fast," Nick puts in.

Kyle shakes his head. "Time to put on your boxing gloves, old man."

"Hey!" Cliff snaps. "First off, I'm *not* old."

"Okay, okay," Kyle relents. "I stand corrected. Come to think of it, I did just read an article about fifties being the new thirties. I'll text it to you later."

"Whatever," Cliff says.

"*Oh, no you don't,*" Jason warns. "More doom and gloom. You hear Kyle, man? Put on your goddamn boxing gloves and *fight* for your woman."

Nick hustles across the deck in a defensive stance. His elbows are tucked in while he air-spars with his fists. "Or else that Mitch will beat you to the punch!"

"It's *not* a competition," Cliff tells him, waving Nick off.

"Easy to say when *you're* the losing competitor," Vinny calls out around a mouthful of grilled chips.

"Who says I'm losing?" Cliff suddenly sits up straighter. "I just didn't get the *chance* to pop the question."

"Hold up." Kyle looks around, squinting into the kitchen through the slider. "Isn't Elsa *here*?"

"She left," Jason tells him as he picks up some tongs and lifts a few grilled chicken wings off a hot plate.

"Yeah," Nick adds, handing Jason two paper plates. "She's probably over at *Mitch's* now. Sitting up on that big deck of his. Watching the stars," Nick muses, gazing at the sky, then motioning for Jason to load up a plate for him. "Holding hands with the professor," Nick goes on. "Maybe more, too."

Cliff stands up and leans on the deck railing. "Enough out of you," he calls to Nick over his shoulder.

"Well, wait. Just wait. And let's look at the things we know for sure." Kyle motions his open hands for everyone to stay put. He leans back against the railing and takes another swig of beer.

"Like what?" Matt asks. He's sitting on the top deck stair and balancing a plate of grilled chicken tortilla on his crooked knee.

"Like that *helluva* Mitch-Elsa kiss—*and* dance—at my diner a few weeks ago," Kyle elaborates.

"Oh, man," Shane says, shaking his head as he still leans forward in his seat.

"Yeah." Matt bites into that tortilla. "And don't forget the innuendo at Kyle's vow renewal," he adds, pointing his partially eaten tortilla at Cliff. "Over that ... that cola cake."

"Don't remind me." Cliff turns around, leans back on the railing and nods. "I know."

So Shane sees it. Cliff's into this tally. "You got something to add, Commish?"

"I might." Cliff sort of turns up his hands. "There was a flower arrangement I wasn't supposed to see. On Elsa's doorstep. Okay, and I had some verbal sparring with Fenwick in the hardware store today, too."

"Well, well," Jason remarks.

Shane tosses and catches that domino. "Seems Elsa might be gauging her options, then. Weighing both sides of the scale." Another toss of that domino. "Cliff, Mitch. Mitch, Cliff," Shane continues. "If that's the case, might help if we get inside her head, boys, to outfox the situation and figure the outcome."

⌒

Which is why, ten minutes later—after Jason drags his portable, foldable whiteboard out of Maris' writing shack—it begins. The Cliff-Mitch Pro/Con List ensues as soon as Jason assembles that whiteboard on the deck. First thing he does? Draws two long columns, labeling one *Cliff*; the other, *Mitch*.

"I don't have to listen to this," Cliff says when Jason caps his black marker and turns to the guys. "It's practically *insulting* to have you people analyze me like this."

"Not analyzing," Kyle assures him as he's arranging various deck chairs in front of the whiteboard. "Just stating the facts, Judge." Once seven chairs are lined up, Kyle motions to them. "Finished heating the last of the cheeseburger sliders. A few more wings, too. So fill your plates, guys, and grab a seat."

It goes slow at first. Everyone's focused more on the night snacks they're working on than Cliff's predicament. But eventually, between bites of grilled chicken tortillas and potato chips, phrases are tossed around.

"Blue eyes versus brown," Nick says.

Jason hands him a black marker. "Start the tally."

So Nick does. *Blue Eyes* begins Cliff's column; *Brown Eyes*, Mitch's.

"Oh, come on!" Cliff barks. "Eye color is *not* a pro or con."

"It isn't?" Nick caps the marker and turns to Cliff sitting in one of those seven deck chairs. He's off to the side, watching this event from a semi-distance. "Remember the brown contact lenses you tried this summer?" When Cliff waves him off, Nick persists. "Why? Why'd you switch eye colors?"

"What?" Shane says, sitting back in surprise. "You got contacts to change ... your eye color? Are you for *real?*"

"Only until he got an eye *infection*," Nick lets on while setting that black marker down.

Something happens, then, seeing this visual. Seeing Nick set the marker on the whiteboard ledge. Jason can't deny it. *Everyone* wants a go at it now—this list-making.

Everyone wants to stand in front of the crowd and denote items on the board. It's like they're power-hungry or something, the way two of them get up just then—Vinny *and* Matt. Vinny's first to the marker and begins writing. While that marker is to the board, and Vinny's arm lifting and swerving, the deck goes silent. Until he steps back and pseudo-dances with an invisible dance partner as the guys read his pro-con suggestion.

Cliff: Slow-dancing vs. Mitch: Shagging

And that does it. That marker circulates from Matt—to all the guys. Each one waits their turn before setting aside their plates of food and taking center stage at the whiteboard on the deck.

And the list grows.

Cliff: Trailer vs. Mitch: Beach Mansion

To which Cliff vehemently responds. "It's not that I can't *afford* a house," he says from his deck chair. "I had a perfectly nice home before moving to this beach community—which keeps me so busy with the *riffraff* and *ordinance* breakers, there's no time for house-hunting!" He stands now and paces in front of the line of chairs like he's giving some closing argument. "Most of my belongings are actually in storage—where I keep a respectable amount of home furnishings. The trailer is ... *temporary*. And Elsa knows that," he concludes, eyeing them all in the flickering tiki-torch light.

Shane raises his hand to talk. "Or," he begins, "Elsa can get pretty comfortable in the grandest cottage on the sand."

When Cliff waves him off and takes his seat again, Nick heads to the whiteboard. "What about this?" he asks after stepping back from his list addition.

Jason shakes his head with the latest: *New England Yankee vs. Southern Gent.* Even more surprising, though, is how the deck turns into some sort of assembly line then. The line at the whiteboard grows; the chairs empty again and again and again; the competition *silently* heats up— except for a few *hoots* and *whoas*—as that black marker gets a workout.

From Kyle: *Connecticut Nasal vs. Southern Honey Drawl* And Matt: *Personality. Rigid and Uptight vs. Laid-Back Chill*

"A hippie vibe which counters Fenwick's job. You'd never guess the dude's an esteemed English professor," Matt elaborates, pointing the black marker to the crowd. "Because, like, he has his doctorate. It's *Dr.* Fenwick!"

Hand raised, Cliff practically jumps from his chair. "And I'm *Your Honor.* I'm a retired State of Connecticut judge."

"Yeah. *Retired*, which sounds *old.*" Nick motions with his beer can for Cliff to sit down. "You've got salt-and-pepper hair already."

"Hair." Matt continues his turn at the whiteboard. *Salt and Pepper vs. Golden, Hip Locks.*

"Well … mine's distinguished," Cliff argues from his sidelined chair.

"And Mitch's," Matt counters as he caps the marker and sets it down, "is just … *cool.*"

"Come on," Jason puts in for good measure. "I mean, the guy has a ponytail."

"Well. Well, write *this* down, Jason," Cliff says, motioning Jason up to the whiteboard. "I was there *completely* for Elsa when Sal died. Even stayed overnight the day of his funeral so she wouldn't be alone in that house. And she didn't even *know* I did that until the following morning. Because I would not have her wake up alone." As Jason jots a few words about Cliff's character, Cliff turns to the guys sitting on the edge of their seats. "Doesn't that count for something?"

"It should, Judge," Kyle says as he spins a chair around, sits and rests his arms over the chairback.

Jason, meanwhile, is busy at the whiteboard. Someone has to come to Cliff's defense, and he has a good one. "Let's not forget this." Jason backs up to show the latest *Pro* written in Cliff's column: *Operation Make Elsa Smile.*

"*What?*" Shane asks.

"Right." Cliff stands again and faces him. "Last fall, Elsa's inn was for sale and her foot out the door," he explains. "*Until,*" he says, walking to the whiteboard and pointing to *Operation Make Elsa Smile.* "*That* idea of mine changed her mind." With a satisfied nod, Cliff returns to his seat.

"Then there's this," Kyle says, walking to the whiteboard and writing his automotive entry. When he sits again, the deck is silent while everyone reads the words.

"Wait," Vinny calls out. "You only listed one on Mitch's side."

"That's because Mitch's vehicle is the only one that matters." Kyle reads his latest words. "Souped-up sport-safari vehicle. Rugged tires, grab bars ... open-air windows."

"Yeah," Nick puts in. "I've seen it all at that trestle. Nothing gets by me. And boy, I've seen Elsa cruising in those wheels, too. Scarf tied around her blowing hair. Big sunglasses on her smiling face."

"*What?*" Cliff turns in his seat. "When?"

Matt interrupts before Nick can answer. "What do you drive, Cliff?" he asks.

"Well." Cliff clears his throat. "A sedan. A respectable sedan."

Groans, *disappointed* groans, collectively rise from the deck.

"But," Cliff goes on. "I restore muscle cars with my son."

Jason leans back and draws a contemplative hand down his jaw. "But do you drive Elsa *around* in a muscle car?"

"No." Cliff straightens in his chair. "Not lately."

"Ever?" Matt asks, then digs into a saucy chicken wing.

Cliff waves him off. "What about time?"

"Time?" Jason asks.

"Give me that thing," Cliff says as he marches to the whiteboard, grabs the marker and starts writing. "I've been with Elsa for a long time now. About a year," he's saying as he's bent there, his arm moving—crossing every *t*, dotting every *i*. He shifts out of the way then. "More importantly, I've *wooed* her." And with that marker? He sharply bullet-points each wooing event listed: *Dinners; Throwing Pebbles at her Window; Roasting Marshmallows on Beach; Kite-Flying; Sunrise Dates.*

"*Ahem,*" Vinny raises his hand to speak. "You said *wooed.*"

Jason looks Vinny's way. In the flickering tiki-torch light, Vinny's nonchalantly leaning forward. Shane sits beside him, one foot raised to his knee, arms crossed. Kyle's in his spinned-around chair. Matt's next in the chair-line, legs stretched out; his hands clasped behind his neck. And Nick's kind of slouched with an arm hooked over his chairback. Some hold a beer; some are eating.

161

But each one of them is *riveted* to Cliff and his whiteboard.

"That's right. I *wooed* Elsa," Cliff confirms.

"Past *tense*," Vinny points out. "Mitch *is* wooing—present tense."

Murmurs circulate through the group until Nick pipes up.

"Yeah, boss. A year into it? You're old news. Mitch is new and *exciting*."

"So … what?" Shane heads to the patio table and grabs a handful of those grilled potato slices. "Elsa's been in a three or four week whirlwind with Fenwick?"

"She's in the swept-off-her-feet phase with Mitch." Kyle holds out his hand for Shane to deposit some chips there. After popping one in his mouth, he looks to Cliff. "*Your* early flame could be in the rearview mirror," Kyle says around the food. "Unless you fan the fire."

"Another thing, Cliff," Jason adds, standing and picking up that black marker again. He shoves Cliff to the side, too. "Don't forget the paltry view when you host Elsa at that trailer of yours." With that, Jason scrawls more on the pro-con list. *View of Supply Shed* vs. *Expanse of Long Island Sound.* "I mean really, Raines." Jason sets down the marker and turns to Cliff leaning against the deck railing. "Throw open your little rear trailer doors to a view of a thicket and a shed? That's a big con."

"Compared to Mitch's view of the sea?" Nick continues. "Stars above," he says, his voice faraway. "Waves lapping below. Massive pro."

All really goes quiet, then. Jason *feels* the silence. There's only the slow chirping of a lone cricket in the yard. The whisper of waves out on the bluff. And that's it.

Finally, someone says into the night: *Hell, even I'd pick Mitch.*

From someone else: *I'm not sure what Cliff's even bringing to the table.*

And another: *Hey, whose side are we on, guys?*

They're just whisperings, floating around. From who, Jason can't tell.

Cliff takes a long breath. Turns and looks out at the Sound past the bluff. The moon's dropping a swath of silver on the rippling seawater there. When he turns back to everyone on the deck, he says, "Well, what about this? I *roll* with this crew. With *all* of you bozos. Been in the fold here for a while now." He turns up his hands, waits a moment, then continues. "Didn't see Mitch Fenwick here today."

"True." Kyle stands and swings his chair around. "Okay, point for you, Judge. So let's get tallying now," Kyle goes on as he walks to the whiteboard. He picks up the marker and adds tally marks to the bottom of each row: Cliff's and Mitch's. Four straight lines, then a fifth tally slashed through the previous four lines—again and again.

"Well," Cliff says while Kyle's tallying, "you all served me up some tough love tonight, that's for damn sure. But you know something, fellas? Maybe I needed to hear what I'm up against."

"That's right, Cliff," Vinny agrees. "It's good to know this stuff."

Nick gives Cliff a fist bump. "Knowledge is power, boss."

"Forewarned is forearmed," Jason adds.

As Kyle methodically moves through the lists, he whispers some of the words. *Personality. Professional title.*

Tally, tally. *Secret trailer apartment. Beach mansion.* Tally, tally. The list goes on. *Commissioner Cap. Safari Hat. Staid. Carefree. Polo shirt. Casually wrinkled linen shirt.*

A groan or two rises as the *Pros* stack up in Mitch's favor.

Before Kyle's even done, he pauses and looks over at Cliff. "Oh boy, Judge," Kyle says, his voice disappointed.

Jason looks from Cliff to the jury seated before him.

With some dejection, Vinny shakes his head.

Matt throws up his hands.

Shane lets out a low whistle.

"Boss?" Nick says, raising his beer can in a toast. "You've got your work cut out for you."

Everyone joins Nick in that sad toast. Cans and cups rise in silent unison. Drinks are taken. No *whoops* or *all rights* ring out into the warm September night.

Actually, Jason thinks, the guys all seem muffled by the realization spelled out on a simple whiteboard on his deck.

A whiteboard accentuated by flickering tiki torches.

A *Cliff versus Mitch* whiteboard—bulleted and tallied to the fullest extent possible.

"Well, it's official," Kyle says. "The final numbers are in. And by our tally here?" He motions to the *Cliff/Mitch* scoreboard and tally marks drawn across the bottom. "Fenwick wins by a landslide."

"*Shit*," Jason says.

Shane stands and walks to Cliff. "You might need this after all, Commish." Reaching into his shirt pocket, Shane gets that scuffed-up domino that Cliff pelted at him and hands it back to its rightful owner. "Little luck on your side might actually be a good thing."

twenty-one

AN HOUR LATER, THE NIGHT'S changed.

Everything about it feels secret now. When Shane veers off the beach onto the hidden sandy path, even the dune grasses whisper. They *shush* and *sigh* as he walks among the sweeping grass blades. Behind him, Long Island Sound's gentle waves murmur. Beneath that heavy full moon, those waves lap onshore, again and again, telling some coastal night secret of their own.

The view that never ceases to awe him, though, is the one he sees when emerging from the hidden path onto the inn's grounds. Elsa's three-story shingled cottage rises against the moonlit sky. Solar garden lights shimmer beside the stone walkway that circles the inn. Globe lights shine on an upper deck extending off the turret. Starfish are propped in some of the lamplit, paned windows. The view is all shimmering light cast against dark shadows.

Which is where Shane stays—in the shadows—as he

crosses the lawn and heads to Celia's guest cottage beyond the inn.

More whispering, then.

This time, it's Celia. She's holding open the screen door to the back porch and leaning out.

"*Shane!*" she calls in a harsh whisper while motioning him closer. "*Over here.*"

He crosses her backyard and steps onto Celia's screened-in porch. Kisses her, too. The thing is, right in the middle of that kiss, Celia starts talking. It's obvious she *never* expected him to show up today and has much to say.

"I still can't believe you're here!" she manages while kissing him. When she pulls back, she touches his whiskered face. "After that checkers game, I didn't think I'd see you for *weeks*. Once you're back on the water," she goes on, taking his hand, "I figured you belonged to the Atlantic."

"Oh, I will. But not yet," Shane tells her as he takes off his newsboy cap and tosses it beside a basket of shells on a wicker trunk. "That ocean will rule my *every* day next week. Well, the sea and the captain will. For now, though? I'm yours."

A pause, then, "And I'm so glad."

Shane tips his head. Her light tone's suddenly grown serious—and he gets a little wary.

"Because I want to talk," she says, her voice dropping.

But Shane can read her the same way he reads the sea. And the same way he knows from shifting ocean winds to pay attention to weather conditions? Well ... Celia's mood just shifted—from a whirlwind of happiness to a serious calm. So he pays attention.

When she reaches for the note he'd given her earlier, he has his answer.

He *knows* why Celia's own condition has shifted—just like the ocean winds. Her own storm is coming in response to his one penned question.

"Shane," she begins, turning to him with that folded note in her hand. She gives him a sad smile. "When I read what you were asking—"

Shane shakes his head. Takes that folded note from her, too. Tucks it in his jeans pocket and raises a finger to his lips. "*Shh*," he says. "*Shhhh*." This time he lightly taps his finger over his lips. His own voice drops then. There's little inflection in his words. "Don't say anything."

Which stops Celia in her tracks. She just stands there looking a little puzzled. A ceiling fan slowly paddles the warm night air in the room. A lantern flickers on the long table against the back wall. There's a lamp on another table between two wicker chairs. The lamp's wooden base is painted a distressed teal; its shade is woven natural fibers; a bulb dimly glows beneath it.

Shane walks to Celia and takes both her arms in his hands. He'll deflect the storm that she was feeling—was bringing to the room. "Celia." He pauses and looks around the shadowed porch. "Aria's asleep now?"

She nods and gives him a small, worried smile.

Which he doesn't return. It's not time for a smile. Not with what he's about to say. "Okay. Celia," he says again. "Just don't say anything. Because when I walked here a while ago? Crossed the beach and cut through the path? I was thinking about that note I gave you—which maybe I shouldn't have done. Kinda kicking myself, actually. And if you interrupt me now, I'll lose my train of thought."

Watching only him, Celia backs herself into one of those wicker chairs near the painted lamp. She sits there and pretends to key-lock her mouth.

Shane looks at her. She's got on the same striped tee and skinny jeans from earlier. And is barefoot. Her auburn hair is down and tucked behind an ear. Casual. Easy. Comfortable with him.

And she's silently waiting.

So he begins.

"You told me a couple of days ago that you were afraid to love me. Or, afraid to *say* you love me. And I get that," Shane admits, his voice very alone on the quiet porch. He drags a hand back through his hair. "After I gave you that note today, asking *what* exactly you were afraid of, a million damn possibilities ran through my mind. That it can never work. That people here would frown upon it." He takes a few steps, wandering the length of the screened-in porch. His fingers brush the leaves of a Boston fern perched on a plant stand. "That Elsa will think less of you." He turns to Celia. "That Elsa's heart will *break*, fearing you'll uproot to Maine with Aria. Or ... or you're afraid that I'll go overboard and you'll be alone again." Shane crouches at Celia's feet. His hand clasps the wicker chair's arm—but he won't touch her. "That it's all too fast. That we're only drawn to each other *because* it's impossible. You're afraid to have me walk *away* from my livelihood." He pauses before saying, "And you're afraid to walk from yours."

He stands then, opens his hands. Moves to the screen door and looks out.

"You're afraid that we're just a rebound thing after Sal,"

his voice continues. Still at the door, he turns and watches Celia across the room in her wicker chair. "That it'll just hurt too much to *say* you love me, because you've *been* down this difficult road before. And there's more. Afraid to have *me* in Aria's life, maybe? Or afraid of the long-distance thing as we go on?" Another pause, then, "Any of those speak to you?"

He paces the porch before looking back to her. "Or is it this?" he asks as he walks closer. "*All of the above?*" he whispers, then reaches down and motions as if unlocking her lips.

"That's it," she says with no hesitation.

"What?" Shane slowly sits in the wicker chair beside hers.

"All of the above, Shane."

"You mean—"

"*Uh-uh-uh.* Now it's *your* turn to lock up."

"Fair enough." Shane finger-locks his mouth.

Celia's hazel eyes glisten in the shadows. Her soft voice comes steady. "Hearing all those reasons to be afraid of what we're doing come from *you*—instead of running through *my* head? It changes things, Shane. You ... you really *get* me. And though you never said if those were all *my* fears—or yours?" She leans close and whispers the rest. "*We're in this together.* And I'd rather have *every single one* of those fears ... than go our own separate ways—and have nothing. So I hope you're really listening now. Because oh, do I have one more thing to say."

Shane only nods.

Sitting in her wicker chair, Celia sits back but never takes her eyes off of him. She's half in dark shadow, half in low lamplight. Her each word is careful and intended. "Shane. I love you *so* much. Love you even more for voicing what I was actually scared to."

He looks from her, to the open porch windows. The night's gone quiet, as if everything outside the porch were listening in, too. After wiping away a tear streaking his face, he looks back to Celia in her chair. And unlocks his mouth. After a long second, he opens his hands to her and talks. "Come here," is all he says.

Celia does. She gets up and squeezes right onto his lap. There's only the creak of the chair, and her quick breath as she sits there and reaches around his shoulders. When she does, Shane cradles her face in his hands, pulls her close and kisses her. Small kisses leaving room for murmurs. For affectionate words.

But even those lessen as their kisses lengthen.

As that's all there is.

As he presses back her auburn hair and touches her face.

As a katydid's slow chirp starts up outside the screens.

As the moon rises higher, casting its silver light onto the porch.

As the distant waves whisper onto the sand while the sea air drifts in.

twenty-two

HELL, THE DAY THAT STARTED off lounging in bed ended with a party.

A damn good one, too, Jason thinks while extinguishing the tiki torches on the deck. As casually as everyone drifted over to his place today, they've drifted off into the night now. Kyle and Vinny were last to leave. After helping Kyle pack up his hot plates and coolers, Jason cleaned up a little beneath the moonlit sky. He swept the deck and collected random paper plates and plastic cups from the lawn. But before he turns to go inside, something gets his attention. It's the barn studio across the yard. Some low lights are on behind the double slider—recessed lights he must've left on there earlier. So he heads that way now to shut them off and lock up the barn.

But as soon as Jason steps into the studio, and smells the faint, musty scent of barnwood, something niggles at him. He's not sure he actually turned *on* those recessed lights today—there was plenty of daylight when he was here printing that photograph for Maris. So with some trepidation, he walks to his drafting table and straightens the oddly wayward stool there—a stool he *always* tucks right up to the table. He moves a few markers on the drafting table and lifts a blueprint-in-progress. Straight black lines delineate rooms; tiny numbers indicate dimensions. Setting the print down, he walks to his L-shaped office desk then, over in the alcove. On his way there, he passes his father's old boat cleats hung on the planked wall.

But still. *Still.* Jason heads back into the studio area. It's quiet; there's only the sound of his footsteps. As he approaches the wall shelves filled with Neil's journals, he looks up the stairs to Maris' loft.

To the empty space where the moose head should be mounted.

"Son of a bitch," he says. Yep, the damn moose head is *gone.* Just … *gone.* Just like that. He backs up a couple of steps and takes a good long look at the glaringly empty spot. Snaps a picture of it with his phone, too, then heads to the double slider.

But he pauses there. Before shutting off those recessed lights, he instead squints across the dimly lit studio to the top of the stairs again. Just to be sure. To double-check in case the lighting's playing tricks on him and the moose is really there.

It's not.

The damn thing's gone.

Someone pilfered the moose head.

So Jason snaps off the lights, heads out the double slider, carefully locks it up and crosses the dewy lawn toward the house.

Glances over his shoulder at the now-dark barn studio, too.

With a disbelieving laugh, he shakes his head and whispers it this time. "*Son of a bitch.*"

~

Maris still can't believe it.

It's why she can't get through fluffing their pillows and straightening their bedcovers after spending half the day *in* bed. No, instead she stops her bed-fussing and looks out the window toward the barn. Someone really did it! Right beneath their eyes, too.

Apparently Jason can't fully believe it, either. He calls out to her from brushing his teeth in the bathroom.

"I mean, they stole our moose head! *Some friends,*" he mutters over the streaming tap water. "And we thought they were all here out of the goodness of their hearts," his voice carries down the hall to her.

"Right," Maris yells back. She's tidying their nightstands now. Setting the brass ship-wheel paperweight atop her neatened manuscript pages; collecting a deck of cards; gathering the messy newspaper sections. "I thought they came to check up on *me,*" she says, tucking that newspaper beneath her arm and bringing a dirty coffee cup and crumb-covered plate downstairs with that newspaper. When she comes back up, Jason leans out the bathroom door.

"Seems someone had an ulterior motive when they came to see you." He does more tooth-brushing, talking around the frothy bristles. "Had a dirty deed in them and swiped the moose head, too."

"*My* moose head," Maris insists, then turns into the

bedroom to straighten up more. But she leans out to the hallway and calls to Jason, "That moose is my good-luck charm! I pat its nose *every* time I go up the loft stairs."

Jason leans back out of the bathroom door. Toothbrush in his mouth, he says, "Someone else is patting it now."

Maris walks to her dresser and folds the olive jogger loungewear she'd changed out of earlier. "Who do you think stole it?" she yells. "Kyle?"

"No way," Jason yells back, still brushing. "He was here all day, mostly keeping the food going. Helped Elsa with her golf cart, too." Jason rinses and spits out the water. "Kyle was too busy and wouldn't have had the time."

"Well." Maris sets aside that jogger set for the laundry. Tidies up her dresser top next. Jewelry. Lip gloss. "What about Shane?" she calls back to Jason.

More rinsing and spitting out, then, "Shane got here too late. And was never out of our sight."

So the moose mystery eludes them. Maris looks around the bedroom at the many scattered chairs. Earlier, Lauren and Matt had dragged them from the spare bedrooms so they'd have a place to sit. So Maris picks up an extra chair and carries it across the hall to the guest bedroom. "What about Cliff and Nick?" she yells to Jason still at the bathroom sink. "*They* could've teamed up and done it."

"But why? They'd have no reason," Jason says, rinsing his toothbrush, then tapping it on the sink edge. "Eh, forget about it." Again he leans out as she's passing by with another extra chair belonging in the front bedroom. "Someday, somewhere, it'll show up," he tells her while pressing a towel to his face.

Maris figures he's right. It's not like they'll *never* see that moose head again—that would defeat the purpose of stealing it. *Someone's* going to want their bragging rights. But *who?* she thinks as she walks to the spare bedroom's windows and looks out onto the night.

"Enough about our ... *friends*," Jason says, walking into the room now. He comes up behind Maris as she's closing the window blinds. "Because I've barely seen *you* this whole night." Wrapping his arms around her, he nuzzles her neck. "We were supposed to spend the day in bed," he reminds her. "Get back more of those lost hours."

Maris turns in his arms and lightly kisses him. Strokes his whiskered jaw, too. "We logged enough today," she murmurs into another kiss. "Don't you think?"

Jason pulls back and squints at her. "No. Not quite." He tucks her hair behind an ear, and tips his head to hers. "So it's going to be a late night, sweetheart."

But Maris never sees coming what happens next.

Never expects Jason to drop down low, grab her around her legs and playfully hoist her up over his shoulder.

"*Jason!*" she calls from beneath her dangling hair as she's hanging upside down behind his back. "Jason Barlow!" she manages while laughing and trying to twist around. "You put me down!"

"Oh, I will," he says, laughing, too. His hands clasp her upper legs and hold on tight. "Come on, let's hit the sheets."

And oh, she feels it as he carries her—hanging upside down—through the hallway and into their bedroom. Flopped over his shoulder like that, Maris feels Jason's strong arms holding onto her as he nears their bed. His hands clasp her thighs; he shifts her body on his shoulder.

Gently then, gently, those hands of his move up to her

hips, her waist, as he gradually lowers her. Still gentle, he slides her down off his shoulder, along his chest and right onto the mattress. They're both breathless; their laughs subside.

"*Jason*," she whispers when he lies beside her on the bed.

He touches her mussed hair. "You feeling okay?"

Slightly, Maris nods. She strokes his jaw, his neck. Her fingers hook the bottom of his old Yale tee, then, and lift it off over his head. She scoots down on the mattress, too, and tenderly removes his prosthesis. Sets it aside on the floor.

But that's not all. Jeans are unzipped; her bra, slipped off; his belt, unbuckled; shorts dropped to the floor. The whole time, kisses are also happening. Deepening. Trailing over their bodies. There is touch, and murmuring. The light is switched off. The sheets are a mess beneath them. They grow a little urgent. Jason moves over the length of her body. Words are few now. Those touches, greedy. Skin grows damp with perspiration.

And yes, they end the day logging another thirty minutes right where they began it—many hours ago—as the sun was just rising in the dawn's eastern sky.

twenty-three

MEASURING TAPE."

Kyle holds out his hand while saying it. It's very early Sunday morning, and he's standing on the top of a stepladder in the old Foley's back room. When Elsa sets the measuring tape in Kyle's palm, he slides the tape open, checks and double-checks the pencil marks on the wall, then climbs down the ladder.

"Good to go," he tells Shane.

Shane sets aside a coffee he'd been drinking, and they switch places. When Shane's at the top of the ladder, he twists a heavy-duty lag screw into a stud—right on the pencil mark there. As he twists the screw in deeper, he's lightly whistling, too. Kyle and Elsa stand back and watch. Everyone's quiet, except for the whistling. Shane glances over at them. In jeans and a tie-front blouse, Elsa's also got a knotted bandana tied around her head. Kyle's in his chef uniform—black tee with black pants—and checking the hanger on the back of the moose head now.

"Kyle," Elsa says. "You're in your work clothes. I hope this isn't too much trouble for you."

"Nah. Sunday mornings are mobbed at the diner, but I've got some time. Don't worry."

Shane glances over his shoulder at Kyle. "You fire up that griddle when you *get* to that diner, man. I'll be your first customer," he says, then resumes whistling while twisting in that screw.

But he glances behind him at the sound of Celia's voice. She's walking into the inn's back room. Aria's in her arms, too. The baby's in a beige ruffle-sleeved shirt and floral shorts tied with a wide bow. *"See Mr. Moose, Aria?"* Celia whispers, stopping in front of the moose head set on the floor.

"Buongiorno, Celia," Elsa says, rushing to them. "And sweet Aria!"

"Hi, everybody." Celia lightly waves her daughter's hand at them all.

"Celia," Shane says over his shoulder. "Aria."

"Hey, little baby." Kyle waggles Aria's stockinged foot. "Morning, Cee."

"There's coffee over there." Elsa motions to a nearby booth.

"Biscotti, too," Shane tells her.

"Oh!" Celia, wearing a loose tee over frayed denim shorts, heads to the booth. "Would you like one, Shane?" she asks.

"Not yet." He looks around for Elsa and holds out his hand. "Needle-nose pliers."

When Elsa slaps them into his hand, Shane turns and

grips the lag screw with them. Resumes whistling, too. Turning the pliers, he slowly twists the screw deeper into the stud. With each rotation, his arm brings the pliers down and around before he regrips that screw and does it over again—all to some vaguely whistled happy tune.

Kyle stands by and bites into a coffee-dunked biscotti. "You're in a good mood, bro," he says around a mouthful.

"Yeah, I am." Shane glances over at the ladies. "Now, Elsa. You got to spill it. *Whatever* came over you two to snag this here moose?"

"Because let me tell you," Kyle adds, "Barlow's going to have it out for you when he catches sight of this."

"Oh … it's just some hijinks between me and Cee," Elsa explains, then sends a wink Celia's way.

Still working on that screw, Shane glances over at Celia in the booth now.

Right as she sends the slightest wink—one nobody would notice—*his* way. "You never know *what* we're up to," she says, settling Aria in her lap.

Shane looks a moment longer. Celia's all smiles today. And rested. He can figure why, too. He's actually *witnessing* the reason right now. It's that Celia and Elsa are softening. They're repairing the rift between them with this whole moose-stealing beach felony. That, and okay … He *hopes* it's that Celia freed herself when she said she loves him, too.

"Now listen," Elsa is saying. "I want this moose to be a *complete* surprise at our luncheon today."

"I heard something about that lunch," Shane tells her as he struggles to give that screw one last rotation into the stud.

"Shane." Elsa walks closer to the ladder and looks up at him. "I didn't know if you'd still be here. Can you make it?"

"Not sure." Shane climbs down the ladder and picks up the measuring tape. "It'd be tough. Have to hit the road early today," he says while measuring the placement of that heavy-duty hook on the back of the moose head. "Shoving off the docks tomorrow before sunup," he says, glancing over at Elsa.

"Well, how about this? Swing by here *early* lunchtime, and I'll have a full meal all wrapped up for you. You can have it tonight after your long drive home."

"Excellent." Shane lifts the hem of his sleeveless tee and clips the tape measure to his jeans. "I'll do just that."

"How about you, Kyle?" Elsa turns to him.

Kyle's leaning on a counter. "What *about* me?" he asks, dunking the last of his biscotti.

"Can you steal away from the diner for our luncheon?"

"You betcha. Texted Jerry to cover the afternoon shift soon as we got your invite yesterday."

"Good, good." Elsa lightly claps her hands together. "But in the meantime," she goes on, walking to Celia's booth now, "don't say anything about that relocated moose. To *anyone*."

Shane hitches his head for Kyle to help him *lift* that moose now.

"We trust you fellas can keep a secret?" Celia calls over from the booth.

"Oh, yeah," Kyle assures her as he sets down his coffee. Bending then, he hefts his side of the eighty-pound moose head. "It'll be so worth it, just seeing Barlow's expression when he sets his eyes on this later."

"Shane?" Celia presses. "You good for your word, too? You can keep our little secret for a few more hours?"

Straightening from his side of the lifted moose, he manages a long look around its wide antlers—directly to Celia. "Most certainly can," he says.

⁓

"How're you feeling today?" Jason asks.

"Mm, so much better," Maris answers from the bed Sunday morning. The curtains are drawn and she's dozing beneath the sheet.

Standing there in pajama bottoms and yesterday's Yale tee, Jason lifts out a clean shirt and cargo shorts from his dresser. He presses them into a clothing bag hooked onto his forearm crutches. "How about the shaking? Any more of that?"

"No," Maris' sleepy voice comes to him. Her eyes are closed; the sheet's pulled up to her shoulders. "Yesterday really helped settle me down. Just relaxing like that."

"I'm glad, sweetheart. Grabbing a shower now," Jason tells her when he turns on his crutches and heads for the hallway. "You sleep in some."

"I will."

Jason stops in the doorway, though, when he hears her voice again.

"Oh, hon," she's saying. "Meant to tell you I put that teak shower stool you bought for Ted's in the shower up here."

"Okay, good." Standing there on his crutches, he glances down the hall, then looks back to her in bed. "But where's the old stool? I liked that one, too."

"I put it in the outdoor shower cabana. It's better than the shot webbed chair you were using there."

Jason, still in the doorway, just watches her drift back to sleep. And thanks God he's still able to do that, after Friday night. Turning away, he catches sight of their framed beach photograph atop his dresser. He walks to it, drops it in his clothing bag and heads to the hallway again. "Going to take an outdoor, salt-air shower actually," he calls, just as his crutches hit the stairs.

"Feed the dog first?" Maris faintly calls back as he makes his way downstairs.

He will, but not first. First, this. First, a stop in the living room. With Maddy at his heels, he turns in and goes to the mantel over the stone fireplace. The dog presses against him as he walks. She laps at a hand on one of the crutches, and circles around him.

"Hang on, Maddy," Jason says when he stops at the mantel. "Easy does it." Leaning on one crutch then, he shifts around some of the things on that mantel—his and Maris' wedding photo; a picture of him and Neil beside it; rustic tin stars leaning against the wall; a carved seagull on mini pilings; hurricane lanterns.

"Maybe there." Jason eyes the mantel, then pulls Ted's picture frame from his clothing bag. The frame is striking with its distressed planks of wood. A silver boat cleat is centered beneath the photograph of him and Maris—fresh out of the sea, hair slicked back, water droplets on their smiling faces. He sets the framed photo on the right side of the mantel, in a cleared spot in front of one of those tin stars.

But the placement has to be just so. Jason nudges the frame over, then turns to his upholstered chair behind him. Gauging the view from his chair, he turns back to the photo and is satisfied. He'll see it from where he sits sometimes, late at night.

Now, though? In the morning quiet, he looks at the picture for a long moment before getting to the dog, the shower, the day.

～

After walking the guys out, Elsa silently watches Celia and the baby from the doorway. Celia's standing and looking at that moose head mounted in the inn's back room. She's slightly bouncing Aria in her arms, too, as she inspects the work Kyle and Shane did.

"They're off to the diner, Cee," Elsa finally says. Nodding to the moose, she asks, "What do you think?"

Celia turns to her. "Well, Elsa. We did it," she says. "We got into trouble together, but good."

"Oh, did we ever." Elsa's carrying a baby seat she'd brought into the room now. She sets the seat on the booth table. "But we're doing something more than that, aren't we? More than getting in trouble together."

Celia gives her a small smile. "You're not talking about Mr. Moose here, are you?"

Elsa shakes her head, walks to Celia and takes the baby from her arms.

"I didn't think so," Celia says.

Elsa's settling Aria in the baby chair. Fuzzy animals and shapes hang from the toy bar looped over that chair.

"Let's take ten minutes, now that the fellas are gone and it's quiet," Elsa says over her shoulder. "Then it's *avanti tutta*! Full speed ahead cooking all morning for our luncheon."

"Okay." Celia walks to the coffeepot on the counter. "There's enough coffee left for a couple of cups?"

"You pour," Elsa agrees, then sits in the booth with Aria. The baby's cooing and reaching for a fuzzy yellow star on the toy bar. "Then we'll have a biscotti truce?"

"Oh, Elsa," Celia says, carrying over the coffee cups and sitting in the booth. "I was hoping you'd say that. That you'd want to talk more."

"I do." Elsa takes her coffee and sips some. "But nothing like a little hijinks first to clear the air, no?" she asks. "To break the ice."

Celia nods. "And it did! I actually had a *lot* of fun doing it." She reaches over and squeezes Elsa's hand. "Boy, have I missed plotting and planning things with you. Which is why I did this, too."

"Celia?" Elsa asks as Celia is digging in her tote. "No *more* hijinks, I hope?"

"No." Celia tucks her hair behind an ear, then slides an envelope across the table. "Only this," she says, nodding to the envelope inscribed with Elsa's name on it. "*I wrote it first thing. At sunrise,*" she whispers.

Elsa opens the envelope and pulls out a pale blue card. She silently reads the verse inscribed and encircled with vines on the front of it. *My world's a nicer place ... with someone as nice as you in it.* The words just about break Elsa's heart. "Celia," she says.

"Open it."

Elsa does. She opens the card to the message Celia penned inside. These words, she quietly reads aloud.

Elsa,

You are one of the wisest women I know. If you felt it wasn't right, or in your heart, to open the inn yet—I trust you. Completely. Something told you to hold off, and we will listen. Sometimes it feels like we've only just started to exhale from this past year.

When the inn doors do eventually open, I'll be by your side. Aria, too. And Sal in spirit—in those beautiful marsh rowboat rides we're going to get approved. We'll fight the good fight together.

So maybe I took a roundabout way to get there this hard month, but I understand now ... and thank you. Thanks for being the very best nonna, business partner (most of the time!), landlord, shoulder to cry on, friend (dear, dear friend)—and moose head co-conspirator.

Love you,
Celia

When Elsa looks up from the card, Celia tells her, "There's more. On the back."

Pressing a napkin to her eyes, Elsa flips the card over. "*P.S. Picked up the cutest pairs of sunnies at Sound View Gift Shop. Let's you, me and Aria grab some more late-summer beach days.*" When Elsa looks to Celia again, she's sliding a gift bag across the table.

"Celia! When did you *ever* do this?"

"Yesterday. On the way home from my dad's, when I was picking up things from my staging shed?"

Elsa nods.

And she knows.

She knows bringing Celia on board as assistant innkeeper was always the right decision. She knows, too, why Sal fell in love with Celia. Fell in love with Celia and her beautiful, generous heart. A tear escapes, then. A little bit of Sal seems to be in this room right this very second. In the golden sunlight streaming in the window; in the dust particles floating in the light like stardust. In the words whispered on a breeze drifting through the window— *Sorridi, Ma.*

Smile.

Celia's fighting tears, too. "I don't want to be mad anymore."

When she says it, Elsa stands to hug her. Her arms are open as Celia slides out of the booth.

But Celia stops—suddenly. "Wait," she manages to say, the word choked on some emotion. "Hold that hug." She turns to lift Aria out of her seat. Holding the baby, Celia walks straight into Elsa's arms. The three of them stand there, lean close, brush a tear off the other's cheek and embrace.

Yep, Elsa thinks. *Just as it should be.* They embrace right there on the creaky floors of Foley's old back room, in the morning sunshine—beneath one badass moose head that's now theirs.

twenty-four

"WHAT A SHAME," MARIS SAYS.

"What is?" Jason asks her.

Noontime Sunday, they're just stepping onto the stone walkway leading to Elsa's inn. The mid-September ornamental beach grasses are golden. Their blades arch high, their feathery seed heads swaying in the sea breeze. And the hydrangeas! Violet-tan blossoms fill the shrubs. White conch shells shimmer in the wood mulch beneath the plantings.

"It's a shame the inn didn't open," Maris says as they stroll the curving walkway. "Elsa turned it into such a magical spot."

Jason takes Maris' hand. "She'll get around to it. When she's ready."

"I know." Up ahead, words are chalked across the walkway in a sweeping, grand cursive. "Oh! Let's see what Elsa's *inn*-spiration is for her calm-down luncheon today."

They approach the large, written words. And slow their step. And stop right in front of the message.

As Maris stands there in her sleeveless navy blazer dress, that sea breeze stirs again. "Huh," she says, then reads the chalked phrase aloud. *"You say tomato ... I say—lunch!"*

"What?" Jason asks, looking at her.

Maris only shrugs. "Tomatoes ... for *lunch*?"

⌒〜

Apparently so.

Jason can't miss it when he and Maris walk through Elsa's kitchen. There's no hiding it. No concealing it. No camouflaging it. Tomatoes are everywhere—in sandwiches. *Trays* of sandwiches that Celia is arranging. There are grilled cheese and tomato sandwiches; BLTs; tomato sandwiches on bread; on sliced buns; on croissants. Triple-decker sandwiches and open-face sandwiches. Sandwiches oozing lettuce, or mayo. Toasted or soft. Then there's a salad: cucumber and *tomato*. A tray of baked *stuffed* tomatoes, too.

Even Matt and Eva arriving—talking and hugging as they do—can't distract from one fact. Some tomato tornado was whipped up in Elsa's kitchen this morning. She and Celia have been very busy.

Jason, Maris, Matt and Eva join Kyle and Lauren already in the dining room. There are more greetings, a *Hey, bro*, a hug with the ladies. Jason pulls out a shabby French country chair for Maris, then sits beside her at the long, wood-planked dining room table. Sun-bleached seashells lean against brushed-silver lanterns on the centerpiece. And the wall of floor-to-ceiling windows beside him? They give a clear view to the distant beach. Blue sky and blue sea reach to the horizon.

When Celia delivers a tray of BLTs on toasted sourdough bread to the sideboard, Jason tips back his chair. Craning his head for a view into the kitchen, he spots Elsa wrapping some food. "Elsa DeLuca!" Jason calls to her. "*You* are a woman of deception."

From where she stands at a counter, Elsa throws him a panicked look. "*Jason* ..." she slowly warns.

And Jason sees it. Sees her eyes saying something else.

Saying, *Be careful now.*

Saying, *Don't mention any secrets. Don't mention Mitch.*

Of course, Jason doesn't. Instead he tells Elsa what's on his mind. "This is *not* a calm-down lunch," he informs her while still tipped back in his chair. "This is a dump-your-tomato-crop-because-your-cart-got-shut-down lunch." He pulls his chair up to the table then. "A clean-out-your-*garden* lunch."

"Sounds good to me," Vinny says when he and Paige sweep into the room.

More greetings circle that long wood-planked table as the newcomers sit, and sip water, and unfold napkins. Elsa calls out from the kitchen to ask if anyone's seen Cliff—who should be here by now. Celia bustles into the dining room again. Her arms hold high a tray of assorted grilled cheese sandwiches. Mouth-watering, *delectable*-looking sandwiches.

Maris nudges Eva beside her. "Where's Tay today? I didn't see her come in."

"Oh, she's watching Aria in the guest cottage."

"And is such an angel to do that on short notice," Celia says, squeezing Eva's shoulder as she passes behind her.

Jason doesn't really hear what they say next. He's too busy motioning Kyle over to check out something *amazing*. There's actually fried *egg* nestled inside those BLTs, with some fancy herb mayonnaise slathered over the whole damn thing.

～

Elsa closes the lid on the last of her disposable food containers and sets it in a cloth tote with the others. Two containers hold a variety of jumbo tomato-specialty sandwiches. Two more *divided* containers hold servings of bruschetta and tomatoes stuffed with breadcrumbs, mushrooms and spices. She turns to Shane waiting near the side door.

"I packed extra," she quietly tells him. "In case you want to heat some up after long days on the water."

"Appreciate that, Elsa," Shane says, taking the tote from her. Meanwhile, conversations hum in the dining room.

"You're not sneaking out the same way you came in, through that side door?" Elsa asks.

"No. I'll stop in there and say goodbye to everybody." He sets the tote on the counter and walks into the dining room with a big wave. "Hey, guys. Sorry to miss the lunch, but got to get going—back to Maine," he says, slapping Jason's shoulder. Shane turns to Maris next, bends and gives her a hug. "Glad you're okay. Both of you," he adds when she squeezes his hand.

"You take care, Shane," Maris tells him as he straightens.

"Good seeing you, all," he announces to the gang, then pulls his newsboy cap from his back pocket and puts it on. "Got my cottage rented another month, so I'll try to get here when I can. For now, I'm hitting the road."

"And the high seas." As Kyle says it, he gets up from his seat across the table and motions for Shane to wait up.

Shane does. He also puts up his dukes and gives a faux swipe at Kyle before hugging him, clapping his back and telling him to watch out for these folks.

And the farewells keep coming. Waves come across the room from Paige and Vinny. One from Celia standing near the sideboard. A quick hug from his sister-in-law, Lauren. From Elsa, too. "Thanks for coming," she says. "Be well."

Shane nods and tells her he'll let himself out. He tips his hat at the room then, before he turns to leave. When he does, there's one last send-off.

"Come back soon!" Matt's voice calls out.

Shane keeps walking away. Because the thing is? None of them realize he's kind of choked up as he crosses the big kitchen alone now. But it doesn't last long, that knot of emotion. Only until he reaches for his tote of specialty sandwiches and hears a *new* voice calling out.

"Wassup, *wassup*, gang?" Nick's asking as he walks down the hallway from the back room. When he gets to the dining room, he clasps his hands on the doorframe and casually leans in. "And what is *up* with that moose head?"

Which is all Shane needs to hear—and to grin—as he sets down the tote, crosses his arms and parks himself in the kitchen to listen in some.

"*What?*" Jason's asking, turning around in his chair to face Nick. "What moose head?"

"*Yours*, man." Nick motions down the hall. "I came in off the deck and couldn't miss that mammal hanging on the wall back there."

"Oh my God, Jason!" Maris nearly spills her chair as she jumps up. *"That's* where it went!"

If Shane could laugh, *shit*, would he ever. But he stifles it and just listens to the mass exodus. Chairs scrape, feet shuffle, voices rise in disbelief. Everyone rushes straight to the old Foley's hangout room—without a glance back.

Well. Everyone except Celia. Wearing a fitted sleeveless camel button-down tucked into baggy cream trousers cinched with a sash, she's standing in the kitchen doorway. Her hair is in a wispy topknot; she gives a regretful, silent wave.

"Hold up, Celia," Shane quietly says as he steps toward her. He looks past her, too, to be sure the coast is clear. When he sees that it is, and hears everyone making a ruckus in the back room, he takes her arm. "We have a minute," he tells Celia as he pulls her aside, out of view of anyone coming. "Probably less."

"Ah. This is it," she says.

Shane says nothing in return. There's no time. Not even a few spare seconds. Because he's using those seconds to cradle her face, bend to her and steal one sweet kiss. Inhale it, actually.

"Fair winds and following seas," Celia murmurs into their brief embrace.

When he hears the words, the familiar goodbye used for sailors, Shane backs up a step and silently squeezes her hand. Celia looks at him for only a second more before turning away and hurrying to the back room—right as he heads through the kitchen to leave out the inn's front door.

"Okay." Jason stands in the back room beneath that looming moose head. "What do you have to say for yourself, Mrs. DeLuca?"

"*What?*" Elsa asks. "I mean, nothing! How do you—"

"Oh, come *on*," Jason interrupts her.

"Aunt Elsa?" Maris asks. "Did *you* do this—or didn't you?"

Elsa's hand flies to her heart. "I'm as surprised as you are!"

"*Deflecting*," Vinny notes.

"So wait, Elsa. You're telling me that you didn't have *anything* to do with the moose in the room?" Jason persists. "In *your* room?"

"I can vouch for Elsa," Celia interrupts when she rushes in. "I was with her *all* morning. We were in the kitchen getting lunch ready!"

"Well, *somebody* here did this," Jason goes on. But he goes on with a slight smile he can't shake. Because somebody here pulled off the near impossible. Really, that kind of bravado deserves kudos. Instead, with *some* gruffness, he says, "Somebody stole that moose yesterday under the *pretense* of caring about my wife. So this actually has a little evil bent to it." He slowly turns and eyes the people scattered around the room. "Anyone talking?"

"Wasn't me," Vinny says from where he's leaning against the pinball machine.

"*Pssh*. Me, either," Nick declares. "Foley's was before *my* time, peeps. I was never in this room back then."

"Yeah." Kyle sits in a booth with Lauren. "You were watching cartoons on TV."

"Kyle?" Jason nods at him. "This have anything to do with you?"

"Me?" Kyle asks, turning up his hands. "I was manning the food yesterday—for *your* guests. Not to mention, I helped you steal that moose *outta* here, years ago."

"Along with me," Matt adds from where he's sitting on a countertop. "So count me out."

Jason turns to Elsa and squints at her. Wearing black lace-trimmed capri leggings with a sleeveless denim tunic, she's standing near the screen door to the deck. Arms crossed, she leans against the doorjamb. "You're behind this somehow," Jason tells her, stepping in her direction. "I just know it."

Elsa shrugs. "Prove it."

Jason looks longer at her because, hell, that twinkle in her eye is undeniable. Oh, Elsa knows *something*. But he's got nothing on her. No evidence. No witnesses. *Nothing*— except that the moose head is back on *her* property. He laughs, then. Because someone—someone *here*—got him. Got him, but good. "All I'm going to say is this," he begins, pointing at each of them around the room. "Someday ... somehow ... that moose head *will* be returned to my barn studio."

"But don't you like it here?" Celia asks.

Jason turns to her sitting with Maris in a booth. "*What?*" he asks back.

"Let's face it, Jason," Celia goes on while standing. "That moose head is part of the *original*," she says, air-quoting the word, "Foley's hangout room you *insisted* Elsa honor." Celia keeps walking, too, stopping at the supply closet before turning to him. "So the moose head is where it should be. Which means … I think this frame is yours now." She crosses the room and hands him the empty gold frame that denoted the moose's absence from these very walls. "You might want to hang it in your studio?"

With a wry grin, Jason shakes his head.

"Anyway," Elsa pipes up as she walks closer to the mounted moose head. "No matter *who* pulled this stunt, I think that handsome moose is back where it belongs, actually."

As she says it, there's a noise. A high-pitched rumbling in the distance.

"Guys?" Eva looks over toward the screen door to the deck. "What am I hearing outside?"

Jason hears it, too. A revving engine of some sort. A sputtering engine. It's growing louder by the second— enough to get everyone forgetting about the moose and rushing out to the deck instead. They all go to the railing and lean over for a better look at the parking area below. Someone's there, sitting on a parked two-seater scooter and, seriously? He's *revving* that putt-putt engine.

Jason squints down at the driver. "Is that Cliff beneath that helmet?"

Right then, the driver takes off his helmet. It *is* Cliff, and he waves to everybody, too. "Hop on, Elsa!" he calls up.

Elsa squints and leans closer. "*Cliff?* What's gotten into you?"

He brushes aside his windblown hair. "Come find out and take a spin around these beach roads."

Celia, standing beside Elsa, gives her a nudge. "Go! *Go!*"

Elsa spins to Celia now. "But lunch! I mean, we have plans! And …" Elsa says, glancing around at everyone

195

eyeing either her or Cliff's scooter. "And we have *guests*!"

"Which your assistant innkeeper can handle," Celia insists with another nudge—a pushier one this time. "Go have some *fun*, for crying out loud!"

Elsa stops and looks from Cliff, to Celia. "I haven't done anything like this since I lived in Milan!"

"Come on, woman!" Cliff calls up, then revs that fancy scooter's engine. "Time's a-wasting. Got these wheels rented for the day."

Again, Elsa looks from Cliff, to Celia, and to Jason and Maris, too—all of them shooing her off. So she touches her hair and turns to the door. "Just let me grab my purse and sunglasses!"

When she's inside, Jason moves along the deck railing for a better look at Cliff's snazzy scooter. It's a sporty blue Vespa with a black seat and padded-leather backrest. There are chrome wheels and chrome trim. And that's about all the time Jason has to check it out. Because Elsa's breezing through that screen door again. This time, she doesn't even pause to talk to them. She just trots across the deck, straight to the stairs. As she's rushing down them, she's also looping her bag over her shoulder.

"*Ciao*, Elsa!" Maris calls out, leaning over and waving.

"You *go*, girl!" Lauren calls next.

Neither of them—or anyone else, for that matter—can take their eyes off this new development.

Every single person is lined up at that deck railing.

Some shield the sun from their eyes.

Someone yells, *All right!*

Someone else gives a sharp whistle.

And *all* closely watch as Cliff stows away Elsa's purse,

hands her a helmet, then helps her onto the bike.

"How do you like that?" Jason says to himself, leaning on the deck railing.

When Cliff gets on the scooter again, he looks up at them all and gives the engine another *putting* rev.

"*Ha!*" Maris says, waving down to Cliff and her aunt.

Elsa blows a kiss up to the deck before giving a wave, too. As Cliff drives off then, Elsa simply holds on tight.

Mesmerized by that zippy Vespa cruising away on the sandy beach road, they all stand at the deck railing and still watch. And wonder where those two freewheelers might head. And wish *they* were cruising on a Vespa this September day.

Until Celia rings a little bell behind them. "Okay, everybody! Lunch is served in the dining room."

Which gets everyone turning to go inside. Celia holds the screen door open as they all file past.

Kyle's just ahead of Jason when they finally turn into the dining room. "Guess the judge put on his boxing gloves after all," he tells Jason over his shoulder.

Jason nods. "Score one for Cliff."

twenty-five

THE GUYS WERE RIGHT.

Cliff knows it now as he drives that scooter. Elsa sits behind him with her hands holding his waist. She occasionally points out some beachy sight, and yells something to him over the scooter's *putt-putting*.

Yes, he *really* needed to up his game.

And coasting the cottage-lined roads now, Cliff's having a damn good time doing just that. Fitted leather driving gloves are on his hands as he steers the scooter through Stony Point. They zip along, the cottages and bungalows a colorful blur beside them. That afternoon, his Vespa *zigs* up sloping beach roads and *zags* down them—with views of rocky crags overlooking expanses of blue sea. He and Elsa lean into the gentle curves. She laughs behind him. Her hands wrap up and under his shoulders as she presses into him and they cruise beneath the midday sun. He toots the horn at a slow-moving golf cart, then whizzes past it.

When he turns onto the Champion Road straightaway, okay, Cliff does it. He breaks an ordinance and speeds all the way down the road to where it meets up with the marsh. Tall beach grasses sway there, all around the blue water channels winding through them. He then does a slow, careful U-turn at the dead end behind the Fenwick cottage.

Oh, and Cliff's *sure* to *rev-rev* that scooter engine before he takes off again. Anything to get Mitch running to one of the multitude of windows on his cottage there. Whether the big man does, or not, is another question. Now as that scooter zips back down Champion Road, the dune grasses on the berm sway beside Cliff and Elsa; salt air brushes their faces. People gather at the end of the boardwalk to watch this snazzy Vespa cruising beside the beach. Finally, Cliff turns onto Sea View Road and parks at one of the lookout areas. He and Elsa get off the motorbike, lift off their helmets and sit on a wooden bench facing a calm inlet. A bank of massive puffy clouds gathers over the blue water, right at the distant horizon.

But the *real* beauty of it all is that Elsa's still laughing as she finger-combs her windblown hair. Her fingers brush back his hair, too, as he tells her his scooter tale.

"Rented it from that scooter place next town over. They actually deliver, so it was dropped right at my door," Cliff explains.

"And it's yours all day?" Elsa asks, leaning into him on the bench.

"Sure is."

"But why, Cliff? What made you rent that cute motorbike?"

"Needed a change, I guess. Wanted to feel the freedom of being on the open beach roads, wind at my face.

Problems behind me. Free as a bird."

They say nothing then as they pretty much just grin from the exhilaration and catch their breath some. In front of them, the bay unfurls to Long Island Sound. Ripples of blue water sparkle beneath the afternoon sun. That growing bank of clouds is majestic against the September sky.

"Well, Clifton Raines? I, for one, am *glad* you got that scooter," Elsa eventually says, propping her sunglasses atop her head. She takes a quick breath and turns to him. Her genuine smile's still there; her honey-highlighted brown hair, tousled. "Because I haven't had *this* much fun in a long time."

Cliff looks at her dark eyes and tucks back her hair. "Neither have I, Elsa," he quietly tells her.

"Oh, Cliff. It feels really good, too." She turns to the sea of blue again. "Forgetting all my worries like this."

"Yep. And the day is young!" he exclaims, standing and taking her hand. "So let's hit the road, woman. Got places to go," he says, leading her back to his peppy Vespa.

"Where to next?" she asks, walking across the green grass to the parked scooter.

"You'll see." Cliff gives the engine a sputtering *vroom-vroom* before they take off again—helmets and sunglasses donned. Stony Point's beach roads are custom-made for cruising, so he zips along a few more. They pass fluttering whirligigs in front-yard gardens. Flags hang from cottage porches. Pots of late-summer marigolds and red geraniums dot front stoops. They wave to a couple out for a walk, and to an older man watering his lawn.

Finally, the scooter *putt-putts* beneath the stone trestle, then turns onto Shore Road. After a few meandering miles, they stop at a local food truck and eat at an old picnic table in the shade of a tree. They devour grilled avocado sandwiches loaded with crispy bacon, spinach, tomato, melted cheese and mustard-mayo sauce; dip French fries into ketchup; sip sodas; laugh in the warm air.

All the while, those clouds keep rolling in. A breeze picks up, too.

Still, after their food truck break, they keep *putt-putting* and scoot over to Sound View Beach. There, they stop at a roadside flower stand painted with peace signs and doves.

Hmm, Cliff thinks. *One-dollar twine-tied wildflower bouquet versus showy spread of doorstep flowers?* Cliff believes he earns another point here for no pretense. Elsa loved it when he surprised her with one of these humble bouquets earlier this summer—before highfalutin Mitch Fenwick was in the gosh-darn picture.

Moseying there, Elsa leans close as Cliff lifts a little, spindly bouquet of black-eyed Susans and purple coneflowers and such. He leaves a dollar in the cashbox, they place the flowers in the scooter's under-seat storage area and take off again—old riding pros now.

And in no time, they're zipping beneath the stone train trestle once more. The guard on duty waves Cliff in—right as the skies open up. A cloudburst lets loose with a sudden downpour drenching them as he speeds along to his trailer and turns into the parking area.

The thing is? It doesn't escape Cliff that they talk and laugh the *whole* time: dismounting the bike, grabbing her purse and the little dollar-bouquet, lifting off their helmets atop his metal steps, opening the steel door and spilling inside the trailer.

"Oh my gosh, Cliff!" Elsa is saying as she drops her purse on a chair. The rain is thundering down. So she just watches it out past the door. Her hand clutches those wildflowers against her chest; that rain drums steady on the trailer's tin roof. "That was *so* much fun, my heart's going a mile a minute."

Cliff takes her helmet and sets it aside with his. When he turns back to Elsa, *she's* turning to him. "Well," he tells her, "I guess we'll have to wait for the rain to let up. It's just a shower, I'm sure. Then we can hit the road again."

"I'd like that," Elsa says. She looks from her still-clutched bouquet toward the kitchenette behind an accordion-style door. "In the meantime, maybe I should put these …"

But she hesitates.

And when her gaze moves from the kitchenette to *him*, Cliff steps closer to her. Wipes a few raindrops from her cheek, too.

As he does, she leans against the wall beside that door. Reaches out with her flower-free hand and fixes his rain-dampened hair. "*Cliff,*" she whispers. Still holding the flowers, her other hand toys with his hair, then cups his neck and pulls him closer. "This was very sweet of you, today. This scooter escapade," she softly says.

Cliff nods. And loosely pins her to the wall. His hands cradle her face now as he leans in and kisses her. And lifts his hands through her damp hair.

Meanwhile, Elsa's fingers? Well, they gently drop those sweet flowers first, before running along his scruffy jaw, his neck.

There's no more talking, then. No more laughing. Everything's changed in this solitary, rainy moment. There's no zipping about the winding roads. No *putt-putting*. No breeze blowing past. There's only the *hiss* of steady rainfall tapping on the metal trailer.

Well, there's that and there's the same breathlessness they had rushing inside from the rain.

Both of them are breathless again—mid-kiss.

It doesn't stop them, though. The kiss just becomes more intoxicating. More physical as their mouths open; as throaty sighs rise; as their hands and arms tangle. Cliff hears Elsa's slight gasp as her arms hook beneath his shoulders and their kiss deepens further—right as they slowly sink down to the floor in a passion more thrilling than that little Vespa ride itself.

～✎

In Maine, Shane opens the patio table umbrella on his deck. He made it home in good time and now needs to kick back before getting an incredibly early start in the morning. The salt air is heavy this evening, lifting right off the nearby harbor. He hears the bell buoy clang, too, as Shiloh sets out paper plates, napkins and a few cans of beer.

"Glad you could make it here, Shiloh," Shane tells him. He slides a platter of Elsa's reheated tomato sandwiches to the center of the table. "Really sorry I had to bail on your family's barn brunch yesterday. But a friend almost got in a bad accident and was pretty shook up."

"Hope it wasn't Celia?" Shiloh asks, snapping open a can of beer.

"No. Folks by the name of the Barlows. But everything worked out fine. All's good with them."

203

"Okay. That's decent."

"Yeah. And when I got sent home with this care package, figured a deluxe grilled cheese sandwich with all the trimmings is a good enough olive branch for you." Shane sets a croissant sandwich on his own plate. "So dig in, Shi."

"Hey, no prob, bub. I get it." Shiloh reaches for a triple-decker toasted sandwich with a pickle spear on the side. Wastes no time biting in, either. "Oh, man. Is Celia the chef?" he asks around the gooey sandwich oozing ripe tomato, melted cheese, mayo.

"Yeah. Celia and a nice lady by the name of Elsa. Elsa DeLuca. She's the grandmother to Celia's baby daughter."

"Wicked good," Shiloh manages while taking a double bite.

"So ..." Shane washes down a mouthful of sandwich with a swig of beer. "Alex get you inked at that brunch? You were next in line at the tattoo table."

Shiloh laughs. "Nah, man. Was a bummah you left—and I chickened out. Big time."

"Aw, come on. You *did*?"

"Ayuh. And Jeezum Crow, boys gave me hell—as they're wont to do."

"Next time, Shi." Shane digs into that cheesy, tomato-dripping grilled croissant sandwich of his. "I'll get one, too."

"Okay. Next time."

"Now listen," Shane says while chewing a mouthful of sandwich. "You talk to the captain lately?"

"Nope. Just got the same message you got."

"*Be on the boat before dawn. Heading out by sunup*," Shane

says as he forks a hunk of mushroom-stuffed tomato off his plate.

"Ayuh."

They talk a little about their day tomorrow. About how many pots the captain figures to set. As they talk, and eat, and toast the next day, Shane's cell phone dings with a text.

"It's Celia," he says, sliding his phone closer and reading the message. "She's hoping I had a good drive home," he tells Shiloh, then picks up the phone and types back. In a few seconds, he silently reads her next few lines. "*Huh*," he says. "They just had a cloudburst there, then a rainbow."

"Better there than here. Especially tomorrow. Don't need the skies opening up on us." As if pleading to some lobstering gods, Shiloh raises his can to the skies before taking a swig of his beer.

Shane does the same, then types to Celia. *No rain here. Sun's about to set, clear sky. Having tomato sandwiches with Shiloh out on deck.*

"Give me that," Shiloh says, reaching across the table for Shane's phone.

Shane just sits back, hands crossed behind his neck, and watches Shiloh type.

"*Hello, Celia*," Shiloh whispers while texting. "*Shiloh here.*"

"Man, you're a slow texter." Shane leans forward and bites into his croissant miracle sandwich, then dabs at some melted cheese on his chin.

"Shut up, bub, and let me concentrate." Again, Shiloh whisper-texts. "*And don't you be distracting my boy on deck Monday, you hear?*"

Shiloh leans back himself, phone in hand, while waiting for her answer.

"What's she say?" Shane asks when Shiloh's eyes drop to the dinging text.

"Says she won't bother you." He slides the phone to Shane. "And promises, too."

Shane reads the rest of Celia's simple message. *I promise, Shiloh. Safe travels to you both.* Shane sets aside his phone, lifts his beer and tips the can to Shiloh. "We'll have a good day tomorrow. Get the job done for the captain."

"Ayuh." Shiloh swigs from his beer. "You and me, bub."

<hr />

Early Sunday evening, Jason's watching TV when he hears Maris at the back slider. Maddy scrambles from the living room to the kitchen, with Jason right behind the dog.

"*Ugh!* I got caught in the rain!" Maris says, walking in with sopping bags of groceries.

"Here," Jason tells her while heading for the door. "Let me get the rest."

"No, you take these." Maris hands him two damp bags. "I don't have much, just one more on the deck. And I'm already wet," she calls back as she goes out through the slider.

"All right. I'll help put the food away," he tells her when she comes back in, still dripping.

Maris closes the slider behind her. "There was such a downpour in the parking lot," she's saying. "A cloudburst happened right *over* me on the way to your SUV! And by the time I was driving home? Sure, the sun was coming out again. But only after I got good and *soaked.*"

Jason looks over at her. She truly *is* soaked. Her high ponytail is sopping. Her navy sleeveless blazer dress is wet and clinging to her. Raindrops cover her face. Hell, everything is dripping—her skin, clothes, purse. *Everything.* "You look like a wet rat, sweetheart."

"Jeez, thanks. And just what were *you* doing inside, so nice and dry?" she asks, opening the refrigerator.

"I hung the empty picture frame Celia *smugly* gave us at lunch today."

"Where did you hang it?"

"In its proper place. In the barn, where our moose head *should* be hanging."

With two cups of yogurt in her hand, Maris looks back at him from the fridge. "*Argh!* I *still* can't believe somebody here stole it."

"Well, I got the frame hung. Made it back here to the TV right before that rain came."

"Rain! Tell me about it." Maris closes the fridge and pulls a container of blueberries from a bag. "The skies literally *opened* up—with no warning! Oh, my clothes," she says, lifting the wet dress fabric, then squeaking across the floor in her wet sandals. "And my hair." She lifts that sagging ponytail. "It's like I just went for a swim!"

"*Tsk-tsk*, Maris," Jason chides her as he lifts a package of steaks from a bag. "Looks like someone didn't listen to her fortune."

"Fortune?"

"Yeah. From our arcade date two weeks ago, remember? On Labor Day? The gypsy in the glass case?"

"Oh, right," Maris says, taking the steaks from him and putting them in the freezer.

"Yep. You didn't bring your umbrella. And the gypsy warned you that when it rains—"

"*Ach*, it pours!" Maris finishes, *with* a little slam of the freezer door. "That fortune was plain old silly!" she says now, swatting Jason's arm. "I just didn't have my umbrella and now I'm soaked." She veers to the sink and gives her long, drenched ponytail a squeezing.

Jason comes up beside her, though. Turns her and pulls her close—wet dress and all. "I kind of like you like this," he says, then kisses her damp face, her mouth. Touches her wet hair. "Come on. Let's go upstairs." He hitches his head in that direction. "I'll dry you off."

⁓

And he does.

But Maris is actually surprised at how quietly Jason tends to her. How he gets really serious as he removes her drenched clothes in the bathroom. How he slowly undoes the gold buttons on her double-breasted blazer dress and peels the fabric from her body. He turns her next and releases her spent ponytail. Carefully, he slides off the wet elastic. Loosens out the damp hair with his fingers. Unclasps her gold star necklace and leaves that on the sink. He takes off her soaked underthings, too, so that she's standing naked on the tiled floor. One by one, he drapes all her sodden clothes over the edge of the tub, then gets a large bath towel from the linen closet.

And oh, that soft luxurious towel. Its every touch on her wet skin unbunches her nerves. Calms her. Jason lightly presses the towel to her face. Blots her wet hair. Lifts an arm and pats it dry. The other arm. Her shoulders, neck, breasts, hips. She stands there practically limp. Outside the drawn window blinds, she hears the slow chirrup of a lone robin holding onto its song as the sun sets. There's the whisper of distant waves sloshing against the bluff, too.

All of it's a tonic—sound, touch.

So listening to those late-summer sounds, Maris' eyes drop closed with the ongoing sensation of Jason's toweled touch. He doesn't say much, other than to tell her how beautiful she is. And to ask if she feels better, to which she only murmurs *mm-hmm*. And he gently warns that, like it or not, he's going to keep checking on her. When he also asks if she's cold, she murmurs again—this time a *no*.

But when he then wraps that towel completely around her and tugs her close, and kisses her, Maris looks at him. Touches his whiskered face. His tired eyes. The thing is? Her heart almost breaks in the silent bathroom. Because after everything they went through Friday night with the deer incident, and everything they *tried* to do yesterday by staying in their bedroom most of the day, well, she gets the sense that Jason's holding that soft towel wrapped snug all around her *just* to protect her.

To keep her with him, always.

That he would wrap that safe, warm towel around her if only to keep the harshness of the world away from her very self.

twenty-six

MONDAY, WAKING UP COMES SLOWLY.

And Jason doesn't rush it. Oh, no. He lets the day nudge him a little at a time. First, the cool September air brushes the skin of his shoulders. The sensation gets him to open his eyes and see the sheer curtains over the windows. A glimmer of early sunlight shines through as the curtains puff like a sail on a boat. The same sea breeze filling the curtains is the one reaching him in bed. That breeze does more, too. It carries with it the cry of gulls out over the bluff. Over and over, their wild and guttural calls echo.

Lying there on his side, Jason just breathes—easy and deep. Eventually, he reaches for the bedside clock to check the time. When he does, though, Maris shifts behind him, wraps an arm across his belly and lies against him.

"Okay, sweetheart," Jason says, stroking her arm. "Let go. It's time for me to be an architect."

"*Five more minutes,*" she whispers, her voice thick with sleep. "For our log."

He gives her that, no problem. Closes his eyes and, okay, five minutes might have drifted toward fifteen. Gently then, he lifts Maris' arm, sits up and reaches for the crutches leaning against the nightstand. Glances at his cell phone there, too. Yep, Monday's begun—in earnest—as evidenced by the early email from his producer, Trent. Jason decides to open it with his coffee later. For now, it's into the shower; get dressed—denim shirt and white tee over olive cargo pants with Maris' custom inseam zipper; put on leg; check porthole mirror in bathroom and skip the shave.

"*Maybe tomorrow,*" he tells himself—dragging a hand along his nearly two-week light beard before heading back to the bedroom.

There's no denying the day's going to be a long one. So at his dresser, Jason collects the things he'll need. "Stopping in the shed on my way out. I'm taking the leaf blower with me," he says to Maris, who's still in bed. It's hard to tell if she's awake, but he keeps talking anyway. "That flip cottage of mine is a mess."

"Your secret cottage?" Maris' groggy voice asks. She's on her side; her back is to him. The spaghetti strap of her satin nightgown's slipped down her arm. "Yours and Neil's?"

"Yeah. Landscaper can't get it together there," Jason says, pocketing his keys.

"Why not?"

"New kid on the crew, I guess. So I'm going to tidy up there on my lunch hour." Jason opens his wallet and thumbs through his money before dropping the wallet in his back pocket. "Got an urgent email waiting from Trent on my phone. Probably something about this morning's *Castaway Cottage* filming. Then a jam-packed afternoon, so I won't see you till tonight."

"Okay." Maris sweeps back the sheet and swings her legs over the side of the bed. "I'm getting up now, too."

After dropping some coins in one pocket, Jason slips his cell phone in another and hooks his sunglasses on a belt loop. "What are you up to today?"

Maris' back is still to him as she sits on the edge of the bed and runs her hand through her mussed hair. "Eva's driving me to the dealer to pick up my car. We'll grab a coffee, hang out some. Then I'm back to the keyboard this afternoon," she finally says, grabbing a pad and pen off the nightstand.

"Wake up with a story idea?" Jason asks while walking closer.

"No. Logging more of our recovered lost hours." She puts the pen to the architectural journal in her lap. "From after the rain last night. That sweet towel time? And ... you know. Afterward?" she says, throwing him a sleepy smile before writing again. "Plus the ten minutes we lounged in bed this morning. Every minute counts."

"Oh, they do, sweetheart." Jason pulls out his dinging phone, pockets it again, then bends and leaves a kiss on Maris' exposed shoulder as she writes. "Got to run," he quietly says.

"Okay. Bye, babe."

He glances back at her as he's crossing the room. "Love you."

The old wooden dock creaks beneath Shane's feet. The sun's just cresting the horizon and casts a swath of pale gold on the distant sea. This early in the morning, the air is redolent with salt, and he takes a deep breath. Fills his lungs with that coastal tonic. He carries his duffel—heavy with lobstering gear and plenty of food. He made sure to pack enough to keep him going for the long day. Because he can't miss what awaits him as he walks to work, either. Tethered to the dock up ahead? The captain's dark green boat. Rows of lobster traps are stacked five-high on deck. Yep, in no time? Shane and the crew will be back at it out on the Atlantic.

But for now, the harbor water sloshes beneath the dock. He passes an early-rising seagull perched on a roped piling. The ornery bird squawks and ruffles its feathers as he walks by. Shane tips his newsboy cap at it. "Mornin'," he tells it back.

And it *is* a good morning. He's finally going out to sea again this fine Monday. He and Celia are solid. Really solid. And the Barlows are doing well. No damage done, car crash averted. Things are good with Kyle, too. Not to mention the helluva time Shane and his brother had stealing that moose head and stirring things up there at Stony Point this weekend.

So, Shane thinks as he passes the little coffee shed on the docks. *This is what happiness feels like.*

"Yo, bub!" a voice calls from behind him then.

Shane looks back to see his buddy Shiloh shouldering open that painted shed's door. His backpack is slung over his shoulder; he's got a coffee cup in each hand. "Shiloh," Shane says with a salute as he waits for that coffee. It's just what he needs, actually. They stop and lean on the dock railing for a few minutes. Talk some about the weather, and wonder if the lobsters will be cooperating this trip. All the while, they down that strong brew to start the day right.

And before he knows it, Shane's tossing his loaded duffel onto the boat's deck, then boarding the vessel himself. Back-slapping and a hearty hello come from Hunter, the other crew member there. Duffels are stowed away. Gear put on—oilskins, black boots, rubber gloves. Voices call out, *Throw the line!* And, *Throttle up, Captain.*

Fast, fast.

Everything's always fast in lobstering. Right away, Shane feels the rocking motion of the vessel motoring through the harbor and making for open water. The repaired engine chugs; the boat leaves a frothy white wake in the harbor behind it.

As always, Shane also gives one last look toward home. Toward his little shingled house near the docks. He stands there and is glad to have a clear head this lobstering trip. The bell buoy clangs; the coast is dotted with the golds and oranges of September's sugar maples. Actually, he hasn't felt this good heading out to sea in a long, long time. Didn't even realize what he was missing the past years. Missing this complete satisfaction with his life.

But hell, it's because life went and unexpectedly surprised him with Celia.

And surprised him with being back *in* with his brother.

Hell, surprised him with the turns of *all* the tides in Stony Point.

Really, Shane thinks with the rising sun, his life is pretty damn full. Filled to sweet capacity now. So before getting to work, he glances out at the wild sea before him. Tips up his newsboy cap and does something else, too. Shane quietly tells the Lord above, *"Thanks anyway, but give any more good to someone else—someone who needs it."*

⁓

Oh, it's so true.

Elsa can't deny it. She's mentioned it to the girls before—Eva, Paige, Lauren. Yes, she sleeps *so* deep on this darn futon. A futon in a tin-can *trailer*, no less! Go figure. She lies on Cliff's futon now. Her eyelids are seriously fighting her own will. Those eyelids do *not* want to budge, but want to just stay closed and have her keep drifting in and out of sleep.

So she does.

The whole time, soft sounds come to her. Kitchen sounds. Pans from the cabinet. Eggs cracking on a bowl edge. The whirring of Cliff's mini juicer squeezing oranges. More sleep, then the sound of those eggs sizzling on a hot plate. And the comforting aroma of fresh-brewed coffee.

That one, the coffee, gets Elsa to turn and open her eyes. Hanging on the wall beside the futon, there's a framed painting of waves breaking on a rocky ocean ledge. Two white seagull statues stand on a shelf there, too. She looks past those toward the kitchenette, but a four-panel room divider blocks her view. Each panel on that divider is made of embossed metal tiles the color of the sea. Cliff once told her it was his way of bringing the sea *inside* the trailer for a coastal feel. Beside the divider, there's that rolling clothes rack—the one she perused in the midnight hour before lifting off one of Cliff's button-down shirts.

"*This did very nicely*," Elsa murmurs, folding back the cuffs on the pinstriped shirt she woke up in. Oh, Cliff gave her some sage advice when she slipped her arms into that shirt and semi-buttoned it up after they were together last night. Said she *really* needed to keep an overnight bag here for times like this.

"Don't ever want you to be accused of taking the walk of shame, Elsa. Like I was," he'd said. Then, lying on the futon with her, he revealed how Nick razzed him for that earlier in the summer. It happened when Cliff left the inn one morning at dawn—*after* spending the night.

"The *walk* of shame?" Elsa asked. "Why? Were you walking funny or something?"

"Oh, Elsa. So worldly, yet *so* naïve. The walk of shame is what you're taking when you get *caught* out in public as you skulk back home wearing the *exact* same clothes as the day before. And—*busted!* Passersby assume you've had a *wild* night of unplanned casual sex."

Elsa simply gasped a quick breath at that, then threw a hand over her mouth.

With a small laugh, Cliff went on explaining. "Nick was *so* onto us, the way he spotted me half-jogging, half-walking to get to the trailer before folks were out and about. Oh, and he was sure to waggle his finger and—in *no* uncertain terms—informed me I was taking that walk of shame. Got me to duck my head the rest of the way home."

"Oh, *heavens!*" Elsa exclaimed, swatting Cliff's arm. "Do people *really* pay that close attention here?"

Cliff only raised an eyebrow at her.

Okay, so she'll find a cute change-of-clothes bag to pack and leave here at the trailer. Which would be fine and dandy—if she wasn't so totally *confused* about her love life. And in her late *fifties*, no less! Oh, *Marone*.

Meanwhile, she hears Cliff on the other side of that room divider. A spatula is scraping a pan; he's barely singing along to a quiet Dino record spinning on the turntable. She listens closely to Cliff's riff on the old standard.

Nothing could be finer than to be in this tin trail-a in the mo-o-orning.

No one could be sweeter than my sweetie when I meet her in the ... mo-o-orning.

Elsa waves away what she's hearing and lifts her cell phone off the nightstand. Because from the sounds and aromas coming from the other side of that four-panel divider, it's now or never. She has just enough time to dash off a quick email to Concetta.

Actually, Elsa's bursting at the *seams* to do this. So much has happened in the past day alone! Abruptly, she sits up, raises the pillow behind her, fluffs her hair, checks the shirt she's wearing and buttons one more button, then begins hunting and pecking an email on her phone keyboard.

Dearest Concetta!

Oh, yes, Elsa thinks then, pausing her typing. *That's exactly how I feel—like an exclamation point!* Uh-oh. She looks from the phone screen to the room divider. It sounds like Cliff's setting the bistro table out in the kitchenette now. Dishes are clattering. So it's back to the keyboard—quick!

Well, things are beautifully squared away with Celia, Elsa plucks out on her phone. *My heart could just sing over it all, having that rift repaired. You were so right, Concetta. One day, I'll also tell you about the moose head involved.*

But ... as for that repaired rift bringing some clarity to my love life? Oh girlfriend, you couldn't be more wrong.

Again, Elsa pauses. From her futon perch, she leans way to the side and strains to hear Cliff scraping food out of a pan, then gets back to phone-typing her Milan confidante.

I only have a minute, but know this. I'm typing from Cliff's futon—after he whisked me away yesterday for a romantic escapade on a Vespa scooter! Felt like I was right back in Italy as we zipped along all the sandy beach roads here. My hands around his waist. Sea breeze blowing. The day was simply ... perfetto!

Gah! Cliff's in his little kitchenette serving breakfast now (yes, that implies what you're raising your eyebrow at), so I must go.

Hopelessly confused in a tin trailer,
Elsa

twenty-seven

"GOOD TO SEE YOU ON the stool, Barlow."

"Good to be sitting on it, Bradford," Jason tells Kyle that morning—before his Monday gets rolling. Dragging a folded piece of buttered toast through a sunny-side-up egg, Jason glances around the Dockside Diner. Every red-cushioned stool at the counter is occupied. Vintage anchors lean against the far wall. Old weathered buoys strung from rope dangle like pendant lights from the ceiling. Tarnished lanterns are propped in some of the windows. Tidy napkin dispensers and salt-and-pepper shakers are arranged on each table, in every booth—most of which are filled with patrons. He's not seeing any evidence of the September slide Kyle sometimes bemoans. Kyle runs a tight ship, as usual.

"What'd you end up doing after Elsa's lunch yesterday?" Jason asks when Kyle deposits a cinnamon cruller on his plate.

"Eat that. It's proven that cinnamon gives you energy," Kyle instructs before crossing his hefty arms and leaning back on a counter behind him. "Now ... yesterday," he muses. "Let me think. Oh, yeah. Still fixing up my new house. And it got cloudy after lunch, so it was a good day to wash the windows."

"Seriously? You cleaned windows on a cloudy day?"

"Bet your ass I did." Kyle sips from a coffee cup he'd poured earlier. "Cloudy's ideal. Because on sunny days? The windows get too hot, and then they streak and make a mess when you clean them. So I got them done yesterday— in the clouds before that rain came."

"Good thing," Jason says around a mouthful of cruller now.

"Yeah. Then had just enough time to put a big bucket in the yard to measure how many inches of rainwater *fell* from that cloudburst. It's for Ev's science project."

"And how much water did you catch?"

"Not sure. Evan's checking it before school today. Fourth grade already, can you believe it?" Kyle waves to a customer nodding to him and leaving a tip on the counter. "What about you, guy? Get those hedges trimmed up nice?"

"Cliff finished those for me Saturday. So I thought about mowing the grass, but couldn't. You know, with the rain. Then Maris came home soaked from the grocery store." Jason drags a hand down his whiskered jaw. "Had to dry her off and ... that was that."

"Oh my God, dude. The Barlows are back." Kyle shakes his head. "Well, be sure to get to that lawn. The yard's looking a little unkempt. Don't want the commish to fine you on his blight ordinance."

"Yeah," Jason says as he stands. "But I got to run now." He shoves in the last of his cruller. "Off to the Fenwicks'," he manages around the food while leaving a few bills on the counter. "Catch you later," he calls out, just before pushing outside through the diner door.

⁓

Cliff's Monday is as breezy as yesterday's scooter riding. After breakfast, Elsa changed into, unfortunately, *yesterday's* outfit. Yes, she put on the same black lace-trimmed capri leggings and sleeveless denim tunic that *anyone* from the luncheon would recognize. So Cliff—dressed in his uniform khakis and black polo shirt with the *Commissioner* patch on the pocket—right away scooted her home on that snazzy Vespa. He zipped along at a good clip so that they were just a blur to any passersby who might witness their, well, their *ride* of shame.

"*Scootering with my girlie when the dew is pearly early ... in the mo-o-orning,*" Cliff lightly sings once back in his trailer. He keeps singing, too, while shoving open one of the sliding windows, then settling in at the metal tanker desk.

Which is when all singing stops as he gets to work. After pulling open a squeaky drawer for a file folder, he begins. First up? The BOG minutes came in from last week's meeting. Once he reviews them, copies will be posted on both Stony Point bulletin boards—always a tense time as a hushed crowd gathers behind him. Residents pore over those minutes as if they're the latest cable news headlines.

So Cliff skims the minutes' details: date and time of meeting; BOG members in attendance; the treasurer's report; citizen-speak complaints—one about reckless kids speeding in golf carts, the other requesting prompt inspection of a questionable fence.

"Questionable," Cliff whispers. *"Sheesh."* The things folks come up with to disguise their fences? He's seen it all as they try to skirt the contentious fence ordinance—as only living hedges are allowed. So he can just imagine this one and jots a note to stop by the offending cottage this week. Back to the minutes now, he taps a pencil on the paper as he quietly reads aloud. *"Need updated residents' email list. Declined tomato stand on DeLuca property."* He stops at that one, *tsk-tsks*, then reads on. *"For next meeting: Gather beach grading permit particulars. Review kayak rack placement on beach after several aesthetic complaints."*

A short while later—after scanning new ordinance requests, and tallies for season's-end tickets issued and violations logged, not to mention recreation and landscape expenditures—he's finally done. The minutes are ready for printing and posting.

But the other tasks piling up on his desk need tending to now. The hurricane safety package distribution is complete, so the paperwork has to be filed away. He'll start with that. And Cliff doesn't even mind the tedious nature of his routine office work today—at all.

Because, *heck*, he thinks as he picks up the pile of papers and taps them straight. *I'm feeling pretty good.*

All it took was upping his game a little. After his Vespa wooing, yes, Cliff feels like a new man. But now he has to plan something *else* with Elsa. Something to keep his game going and stay ahead of, well, of Mitch Fenwick.

That thought has Cliff walk past the accordion-style

door to a small chest of drawers near his futon. Opening the second drawer, he pulls out a velvet box. It's been two weeks since he bought Elsa's wedding ring. Sitting on the futon, he opens the box and looks at the ring. Its emerald-cut diamond in the center is flanked by a diamond baguette on each side. And each stone just glimmers.

"*Nothing would be sweeter ... than to see this on her finger—*" Cliff vaguely sings, stopping when a truck's *beep-beep* back-up alarm sounds. He hurries to a window and sees it's the scooter company arriving to pick up his rented Vespa.

So Cliff scoops up the keys off his kitchenette counter, collects the two helmets off his tanker desk, and—whistling now—opens the trailer's steel door and heads outside.

⌒⌣

Jason parked a block away from the Fenwick cottage just so he could get in a beach walk. He'll be filming in some demo'd areas later, so he's got on work boots—also good for walking the packed sand on the driftline. A wind's been picking up today. A stiff sea breeze. When he's right at the water's edge, that wind really messes with him. It tousles his hair, ripples the denim shirt he's got on. He keeps walking, cuffing his shirtsleeves and looking across the beach to the dune grasses on the berm. That gusty wind randomly flattens those wild grasses there. And the sight of it has Jason drop his head and briefly close his eyes. Finally, he turns and just looks out at Long Island Sound. It's dark blue this morning under changing skies. And that steady breeze whips the waves into a mini frenzy—much like they're whipping around the sweeping dune grasses.

223

"*Ah, Dad,*" Jason whispers, shaking off a memory. He touches his father's dog-tag chain around his neck before heading to the Fenwick cottage. There's no putting it off—it's time to get to work. As he crosses the beach, more dune grasses rise behind Mitch's cottage. The grasses rustle in the wind, bend, rise up again. A few large pieces of gray driftwood—long ago washed ashore—are in the sand there, too. Jason takes it all in before climbing the stairs to the cottage deck.

Mitch is sitting at a patio table shoved over to the side. Wearing a loose tee and cuffed jeans, he's bent over his cell phone. "Be right with you, Jason," he distractedly calls over. "Just have to text a line or two to someone."

Jason nods and leans against a railing there. He's close enough to hear Mitch quietly talk out the words he's typing on his phone.

"*Late Tuesday afternoon works for my cooking lesson … Will have a big pot ready on stove.*"

When Mitch pauses, Jason takes a few steps away and turns toward the splashing waves below. But he catches a little more of some planned meetup apparently going down.

"*Oh!*" Mitch says, typing again. "*You bring your tomatoes. I'll supply the aprons.*"

All Jason can do, still turned away, is roll his eyes. *Hell,* he thinks, too. *Elsa, Elsa. What are you doing?* But … he lets it all go. It's not his place to tell Maris' aunt how to live.

"Jason, my man," Mitch says when he strolls over. After nudging up his safari-style hat, he shakes Jason's hand.

"Good to see you, Mitch," Jason tells him from the railing.

"Likewise." Mitch leans back against the railing, too, and looks at his imposing cottage. It's surrounded with some scaffolding, some propped-up ladders, some sawhorses here and there, some buckets of tools. "Ready to get to it?" Mitch asks.

"In a minute." Jason draws a hand along his scarred jaw. "Listen, Mitch. I wanted to catch you first and let you know some personal news."

"Personal news? Everything okay, my friend?"

"It is now. But something happened that affects your offer to edit Maris' manuscript."

"Oh?"

Jason nods. "Unfortunately, she has to postpone your first meeting. The one when she's supposed to drop off the book's early chapters?"

"Something happen?"

"Almost. She had a close call, car versus deer."

"Mercy me!"

"Yeah. But she's fine. Happened Friday night. A deer bounded out in front of her car really unexpectedly. So she lost control of the vehicle for a spell and, you know, it really shook her up."

"You, too, I'll bet?"

"Did it ever. I was actually following behind her and witnessed the whole thing. Between you and me, there were a few seconds when it looked like things could go either way. But she recovered control and pulled to the side of the road."

"Thank God for small miracles, Jason."

"Big miracle, this time. For me, anyway. So ... Maris is sort of taking a few days to catch her breath and—"

"Two things, guys," Trent interrupts, raising his hand to them as he's come out of nowhere and crosses the deck now. "One, Mitch. Window people are inside. They need some design decisions on trim work, pane grids. And Jason?" Trent goes on, turning to him now. "Let's get you in there, too. I'd like some footage with you assisting." He glances at his watch. "And ... really? We're ready to get started."

"We'll talk more later, Jason?" Mitch asks as he turns to head inside.

"You bet. But hold up a sec," Jason tells Mitch, then looks to Trent talking now with the cameraman, Zach. From the raised deck, Jason also grabs another look out toward the choppy water. That sea breeze is still kicking around pretty strong. "Hey, Trent," Jason calls out.

Trent looks over at him. "Clock's ticking, guy."

"Yeah, well. Hear me out on something, would you?"

Trent tosses up his hands as Jason approaches him.

"With this wind blowing, I've got a little story in mind for a segment. Something off the cuff." Jason takes off his sunglasses and squints at his producer. "That work for you?"

Camera gear in tow, Zach's standing there ready to film. "Come on, Trent," he says, lifting the camera to his shoulder. "Let's see what Barlow's got."

"All right." Trent looks at his watch again. "All right. Off the cuff's good. Keeps things fresh. Let's do it."

So they all take their places on the Fenwicks' upper deck. Jason indicates the spot at the railing where he'd like the segment shot. Zach, the gaffer and the sound people set up around him. Trent stands back, arms crossed, and watches. Mitch stands beside him, leaning an arm on the deck railing as he takes this in.

When everyone goes quiet, Trent gives the order. "Okay. Roll camera!"

⌒〜

"Landscape is crucial to architectural design," Jason says when the filming begins. As he talks, that wind lifts his wavy hair. "When I start a project, one of the *first* things I do is walk the surrounding land, take notes, photograph landscape details. The structure *has* to fit in with existing plantings, with the slant of the ground, with natural sight lines. Not vice versa. It's nature first—the building second. Like here," he says, motioning to the sweeping beach grasses surrounding the rear and side of the Fenwick cottage. Beyond those grasses, the marsh stretches out in winding pools of blue water and more grasses—windblown now. Zach moves beside him and films the seascape, the beachscape, as Jason continues.

"In architecture, I'll *use* landscape ... to control light. Or heat gain. To visually extend a building's interior to outdoor space. But equally important," he goes on, walking the wraparound deck, "is landscape's influence on *us* as human beings. The effect the landscape has on our emotion runs the gamut. And that's a critical lesson my father taught me and my brother, Neil, one windy day many years ago. A day just like this. Dad checked up on us when we were crabbing for blues on the banks of the marsh. The wind skimmed off the sea like it is today. It got those marsh grasses unfurling and flattening around us. My brother and I were just youngsters at the time—ten and twelve, maybe. But we'd been hearing my father's Vietnam war stories throughout our childhood. Always, *always*, they were told with a lesson. A message. A nudge to growing up." Jason stops then, and faces the wild dune grasses leading to the distant marsh behind the cottage. Leaning his elbows on the deck railing, he feels the stiff sea breeze on his face, and moving his hair.

Finally, Jason turns and tells his father's story to the camera.

———

My father used to say that when he was in 'Nam, the rhythmic thump of helicopter blades was a mighty thing. That powerful thump-thump-thump was so deafeningly loud, it swallowed most other sound. Insect buzzings and whistlings were gone. Bird and animal calls, too. There was only that chopper's constant beating of the air, over and over and over, relentless in its tempo. But, Dad explained to us that day in the marsh, those drumming blades did something else, too. Something sinister he never saw coming. Jason motions to the windblown, now-flattened marsh grasses behind the Fenwick cottage. Zach is filming beside him, and he shifts the camera's focus to the marsh.

My father's arrival in 'Nam? Getting dropped in that jungle land ten thousand miles from home? It went like this, Jason continues. *It prepared him in two minutes flat for what he would be up against during his entire tour of duty. When the helicopter bringing them in descended, those spinning blades flattened all the wild grasses in the patchy field where they were let off. And that sight stayed with my father,* Jason explains. *The force of the wind generated by that hovering bird? Like here today,* Jason adds, *it leveled the grasses. Flattened the landscape. And … bingo, he told my brother and me. That made my father and his comrades easy targets.*

Jason gets a wry smile and shakes his head now. *You see, Dad went on, in 'Nam, there was something else happening as they started disembarking that bird. As they were loaded down with gear on their backs. Something else as they jumped out to the field. Something more than the thundering chopper blades blowing like mad and flattening the grasses. There was another sound. And it took a moment for my father to fully grasp what else he was hearing. After taking a long pause in the marsh, Dad told Neil and me.*

Enemy fire, he said. He heard it. He felt it whipping by. Yep. Welcome to Vietnam.

My father stood in that chopper doorway just a kid full of piss and vinegar, and by the time his boots hit the ground? He was a man dodging gunfire. Believed his life would be over one day in—until some seasoned soldier wildly motioned him where to take cover.

And we knew, then, my brother and I, Jason says, nodding to the wavering marsh grasses. *We knew that the blowing dune and marsh grasses here, at Stony Point, triggered some pretty powerful flashbacks for our father. With the wind skimming just right off Long Island Sound, he could just as easily slip right back into the Southeast Asian jungle. Just as easily be jumping out of the chopper—to enemy gunfire aimed at his life.*

Jason still leans on the deck railing and watches the wildly blowing marsh grasses. He feels, too, that steady sea breeze blowing the fabric of his shirt, his hair. Finally, he glances at the camera. *We also knew then, me and Neil,* he says, *why on really windy beach days, Dad would turn to another landscape. One he customized to fit his life, his home here, with a stone bench his own two mason hands built. A bench atop a seaside bluff. He'd sit*

229

out there alone for hours sometimes on those blustery days. The wind would lift his hair, move his shirt. And he'd calm his panic, his beating heart, by looking out at only the blue sea. That bench he built facing the water was his remedy for what we now might call PTSD. Jason takes a long breath of the salty air. *My dad died a few years ago, and honestly? I miss him like hell. So that's why I also prioritize the use of landscape for comfort, and for calm, too. It's always with thoughts of my father.*

Everyone is silent around Jason. The construction workers. Film crew. Mitch, Trent.

Silent.

Zach films a little longer *in* that silence. The only sound that would be picked up is the September wind lifting off the sea—much like the wind generated by those chopper blades in 'Nam—flattening the dune grasses, and moving those marsh grasses in an undulating wave of green.

twenty-eight

THE DAY WASN'T AS LONG as he'd thought it would be.

But Jason's just as tired.

When he gets home late Monday afternoon, he opens up the shed and puts away his leaf blower. Grabs the old push broom while he's in there and sweeps out the neglected corners, some cobwebs. Late-day sunlight shines into the shed. Dust particles float as he sweeps. The stiff broom bristles swish, again and again, over the wood floor. Finally, he sweeps the accumulated dirt pile out the door and into the grassy yard. That done, he coils a garden hose in big loops, then hangs it on a high hook on the shed's side wall. He putzes here, there. Winds up an outdoor extension cord and sets it on a shelf. Tips his wheelbarrow up on its front wheel and leans the whole thing out of the way against the rear wall. Lifts a limp green rain poncho off a nail, too, and shakes the poncho out in the yard. Hangs the ladder Cliff used to trim the hedges, balancing the ladder on large wall hooks. Looks around, wipes his dusty hands on his pants, walks out and locks up the shed door.

This morning's wind has faded. The sea air is calm. The low sunlight, golden. Jason crosses the backyard to Maris' shingled writing shack and quietly stops in the open doorway. Streaks of wood grain show through the shack's white-painted walls. Vintage baskets and jars lining a shelf are filled with salt-coated shells and faded sea glass. The dog's asleep beside an old cot; Maris types away at her laptop. Wearing faded cropped jeans and a black tee, her back is to him. More seashells are scattered around her work area. Jason finally gives a one-two knock on the open door. When he does, Maddy jumps up from where she was dozing and circles his legs, licks at his hand.

"Hi, hon," Maris says over her shoulder. Her manuscript papers are scattered about; a tarnished hurricane lantern is lit nearby; sand falls through the flipped pewter hourglass. "You're home early."

"Little bit." Jason pats Maddy's head as he talks. "You're writing, I won't bother you."

"Was there something you needed?" Maris asks, turning in her chair—but clearly distracted by the intense creating she just pulled herself away from.

"No." Jason smiles, gives a wave and backs into the yard. "I'll be in my studio for a while."

"Okay." Maris promptly gets back to her work. "I'm just wrapping up a chapter."

"And how's it going?" Jason calls, pausing there in the yard.

"Good. The words are rolling," she answers without turning. All he sees is her low ponytail hanging over her

232

back. A light knitted shrug is draped over the chair. And her hands are going at that keyboard.

So Jason whistles for the dog to follow him and walks to his barn studio beside the shack. The studio's a complete contrast in architecture from where Maris is working. One building is a brown-planked New England barn, the other a silver-shingled fishing shack. But weathered buoys hanging from both structures' outside walls connect them aesthetically.

Inside the barn, the faint scent of old tools and wood dust meets him. Sunshine drops through the skylights. He heads to his big office desk where a pile of mail's accumulated. Some recent architectural sketches are there, too, weighted down with engineering scales. Maddy scrambles up the loft stairs and lies there with her muzzle beneath the railing—her regular spot from where she keeps an eye on him. Settling into his padded office chair, Jason picks up a letter opener and slides his pile of mail closer. He spends the next fifteen minutes opening bills and paid customer invoices. He logs the enclosed checks and continues on. There are solicitations to join architecture associations. Some catalogs of architect tools and supplies.

When Maris finally wanders in, Jason pauses. He's leaning back in his chair; his feet are propped on his desktop; a few more envelopes are in his hands.

"I'm done for the day," Maris tells him, then clears a space on his desk and sits on the edge of it.

"Me, too," Jason says, setting aside his mail and watching her. "By the way, I talked to Mitch this morning."

"You did?"

Jason nods. "At his cottage before filming began. Mentioned the deer incident and let him know you had to

233

postpone your chapter-review meeting."

"I hope he didn't mind?"

"No. Just tell him whenever you're ready. All's good."

"Perfect," Maris says. "I feel better knowing he's okay with a little wait."

They talk some then, about the missing moose head. And the lame empty picture frame hung in its place. And about who orchestrated the whole moose heist for Elsa.

"Because you just *know* Elsa was behind it," Jason says.

"Well, it *did* end up at her place." Maris leans her hands back on his desk now. "But Elsa couldn't lug that thing. So it *had* to be one of the guys who actually did it."

"Hm. Maybe I should install one of those security cameras in here."

"Not a bad idea," Maris agrees. "But anyway, for now?" she goes on, suddenly standing and taking his hand. "The heck with that and take a beach walk before dinner?" She gives a tug. "Get more of our lost time back?"

Jason lifts his feet off the desk and rolls his chair in. Looks over at Maris standing there. She tucks back a strand of hair escaped from her low ponytail. Her star necklace glimmers in the V neckline of her black tee.

"A walk on the beach with you?" he repeats, right as Maddy scrambles down the loft stairs. "You bet."

~

Ah, hell.

Sometimes Jason's really conflicted about his version of paradise. Typically, it's Sunday mornings lingering in bed with Maris.

But this? This gives that one a run for its money.

This pink horizon over a steel-blue calm sea.

This salt air lifting off the water and leaving the slightest touch on his skin.

This wave after small wave making faint splashes on the sand.

But more than any of that?

It's Maris walking beside him. Leaning into him. Jason feels her hook a finger through one of his belt loops. Her voice is soothing as they walk the packed sand beneath the driftline.

Oh, his breathing is easy, too; his body, relaxed.

Maddy found a driftwood stick and trots ahead of them. Her paws splash in the receding waves as she clamps that stick in her head held high.

It's enough. Could be paradise.

Still, Maris picks up on something. Something he's not said. Not let on. He knows it with her remark then.

"You're a little quiet," she says, brushing his jaw as they walk side by side.

Jason takes a long breath of the salty air. Yes, this is beautiful—this walk with Maris. But life, cruel life. Isn't there always something else? Some slight emotion, memory, that keeps things real. "My father's been on my mind today," Jason admits.

"Really?"

He nods. "We filmed a *Castaway Cottage* segment this morning that had a connection to him. Trent actually loved it. Said the different angle I bring is what sets the show apart from others."

"What was it about?"

Jason takes a few silent steps. His denim shirt hangs open over his white tee and cargo pants. When Maris reaches over and turns his face toward hers, he takes her hand and kisses it before going on. "You know how it was windy here earlier today?"

"Yes! I had to put a beach rock from one of Neil's baskets on my manuscript pages. They kept blowing around!"

"Right. And when I was at the Fenwicks' with the crew? That wind was flattening the marsh grasses, bending them right over. And it reminded me of a story my father told my brother and me years ago. So I stood on Mitch's deck, with the marsh grasses blowing behind me, and told that story to the camera. It was about how, for my father, the wind here triggered flashbacks of his getting off the choppers in 'Nam. *That* wind—from the propellers— would swirl and flatten the tall grasses there. But once, early on, he had to hit the ground out of the chopper and run like hell. Land and run—from enemy fire directed right at him."

"Oh, Jason." Maris reaches for the gray chain hanging on his white tee. Her fingers touch the Vietnam War dog tags on that tattered chain. "*Your father was so brave. Wish I got to know him,*" she softly says. "He meant so much to you." Her ponytail hangs loose; her smile is gentle. "But I only knew him in passing, during my summers here."

Jason slips an arm around Maris' shoulders and holds her close as they walk the beach again. The western sky is red at the horizon; twilight casts long shadows on the sand. A lone seagull swoops low over the calm water. "I wish Dad got to know you, too," Jason tells her, then kisses the top of her head. "He'd have loved you, sweetheart."

twenty-nine

THIS IS ALL MARIS WANTS.

This sitting here at their gabled house by the sea. Sitting outside on the front porch. Sitting with Jason after a beach walk and dinner on a mid-September day. The evening light is dusky; the sky, silvery blue. Maris sits there in a brown Adirondack chair. Soft illumination comes from the wall lantern mounted beside the screen door. Recessed lights glow in the porch overhang. She looks over her shoulder through the paned window beside her. Lights are on inside the house, too. The foyer is lit up this evening, as is the entire front hallway.

Because *life* is inside. Jason is there, somewhere in the kitchen while she waits for him on the open porch. Maddy lies nearby at the top of the three wide steps leading down to the dewy lawn. A piece of driftwood is clamped between the German shepherd's paws as she gnaws on the gnarled stick. There's a whole supply of driftwood beside her, actually. This summer, Jason set a square wooden box on the porch. The box holds the salty driftwood pieces that the dog carries back from their beach walks. Sticks of grays and browns are stuck in that box in every random direction.

Right in front of the porch, an overgrown hydrangea bush is laden with so many heavy blossoms. Around the shrub, evening's shadows fall on the green lawn. All of it— the late-summer colors, the scent of the salt air, the setting sun, the sea damp—all of it goes into their lost-time log. Jason's architectural journal is open on Maris' lap, and she puts her pen to the page now. While sitting in that porch chair, she jots all the sensory details around her. Logs that half-hour beach walk she took with Jason before dinner. Notes how she listened to him talk about his father in such a way that she heard his longing. It's obvious how much Jason misses him sometimes.

As she's writing, the screen door squeaks open. Jason walks out carrying two glasses of wine and her knit shrug. So she sets her journal and pen on a small table there and takes a glass from him.

"Oh, wait," Maris says, quickly setting down her wine.

"What's the matter?" Jason drops the light sweater over her shoulders before settling in the Adirondack chair beside hers.

"Well." She lifts that journal again. "I'm trying to make a dent in our five hundred and four lost hours." As she's writing, she whispers her latest entry. "*Sipping wine on porch, late-summer evening.*"

"Sounds really good," Jason tells her. "Give it an hour, at least."

"Okay." Maris sets aside the journal and picks up her

wine again. "Another hour in the books."

And they fill that hour with small talk.

Their voices grow quiet as the sun sets and night approaches. Darkness tiptoes in.

The lamplit screen door and paned windows grow more golden.

The big maple tree towering over the house becomes nothing more than a hulking shadow.

Jason shifts his chair closer to hers.

A mist rolls off the sea.

〜

Shane's hands are shaking.

Shaking like hell, actually. It's evening and dusky shadows have dropped over everything. He stands there on the granite step at the front of his Maine house. His duffel is at his feet. The screen door is propped open behind him. But he struggles to get the key into the deadbolt lock of the wood interior door. His hand trembles enough that he's slightly off in his aim—the key scratching just above.

He tries again and doesn't come close.

Tries again.

Misses again.

His shaking actually gets that key ring dropping right out of his hand. When he picks the keys up from where they fell onto his duffel, the screen door slams shut. For Christ's sake, you'd think he's drunk. Anyone seeing him wavering at his door in the twilight would think it.

He's not.

"*Shit*," Shane whispers, holding the screen door open

239

with his booted foot now. He takes a long breath of the thick salt air. *"Focus."*

This time, it works. Somehow, he gets that key inserted into the lock and turns it, then opens the heavy wood door. Picks up his duffel, goes inside, closes the door and stops right there.

His house is dark. Quiet, too.

He blows out a long breath. Doesn't move, though. For several moments, he just drops his head, then looks around and turns on a table lamp at the front window. His happiness jar is on that table, too. A tiny candle is in it, along with some tangled dry seaweed. Smooth skimming stones are set in the jar's sand. Kyle's flattened nickel is there. Celia's sea glass pieces shimmer.

Well. Wouldn't Shane like to sweep that damn jar off the table right about now.

Instead, he tugs at the collar of his tee, then throws open that front window for some air. Stands there, bends and leans his hands on the sill, and breathes. In … and out.

And again.

Finally, his booted feet heavy on the floor, he hefts his full duffel into the kitchen and drops it on the wooden table. Hooks his newsboy cap onto a chairback. Cuffs the sleeves of the khaki button-down he's wearing open over his tee and jeans.

He's on autopilot now—his routine the same as any other day he gets home from work. He washes his hands. Empties out his lunch sack—today, untouched. Wrapped sandwiches in the trash, uneaten apple back in the fridge, snacks and napkins on the counter, ice pack in the freezer. He puts the lunch bag in a cabinet. Pulls a zip sweatshirt out of the duffel and hangs it on a hook near the back door.

A back door that he opens and pushes through out onto the deck there.

Because this *isn't* like any other day.

Rockport Harbor is off in the distance. The sun's set, but dock lights are on. Vessel lights, too. The lights reflect off the black harbor water. And even though it's dark, seagulls call. They're always there, day or night, trailing the lobster boats for discarded bait. The birds' lonely *caw-caw-cawing* carries on the damp sea air.

Shane paces his deck. Back and forth.

Back and forth.

"*Jesus Christ,*" he whispers. "*Seriously? This is what You had to do today?*" he asks the night sky. His fingers slide along the length of his tee collar as he can't get a full breath. Which only makes him sweat. A bead of perspiration trickles down his temple. Being outside isn't helping, so he goes back into the kitchen and sits at the table. With his elbows on his knees, he just sits alone there.

Inhales.

Sits up and drops his head back.

Goes to the sink—nearly toppling his chair as he does— and tosses handful after handful of cold water on his face. He feels like he's about to be sick.

"Damn it. Damn it. *Damn* it," Shane says, swiping up a coffee cup from the dish drainer. He joggles the cup before heaving it across the room to the far wall. Heaves it for all he's worth. When the ceramic cup shatters, he goes back to the front door. In, out, where's there to go? How does he do this? He whips the wood door open and stands at the screen door. Crosses his arms, leans on the doorjamb and looks out. Yep, his pickup is parked on the gravel driveway. Overgrown geraniums spill from the flower box beneath the front paned window. Surely there's some mail in his mailbox. Everything fucking normal-looking.

But it's not normal. It's *not*.

He looks toward the hallway off the living room. Maybe he'll just go to bed. Sleep off the God damn bitch of a day.

As if he can sleep. As if painful visions won't haunt him behind his closed eyes.

So instead? Shane looks around and returns to the kitchen. His booted feet crunch over the broken cup shards. He keeps walking, though, to the table—where he fishes his cell phone out of his duffel. Blindly, he thumbs through the phone's contacts.

"*Barlows, Barlows,*" he whispers while scrolling up and down through names he just can't see straight. He squeezes his eyes shut, swipes at his damp face, then scrolls the names again. "*Jesus, where the hell's the Barlows?*"

~

Jason swirls what's left of the wine in his glass. The day's been good. Lord, how he's missed this. Missed living like this. Missed sitting on the front porch with Maris at day's end. The sound of distant waves breaking on the bluff reaches him now. Crickets begin a slow chirp. And just then, from inside the house, a cell phone rings.

"That's yours," Maris says, reaching over and touching his arm. "You going to get it?"

"They'll leave a message." Jason waits as the phone rings again inside. "I'll check it later."

Once the ringing stops, they talk more. Maris tells him how some of the guys thought they should hang a plaque on the front of the house.

"A plaque?" Jason asks.

She nods. "Eva and I heard them talking Saturday night, when everyone was here. They said it should be some coastal emblem, like a metal crab. And our initial—B for Barlow—would go between the two curved claws."

They consider the idea, debating crab, seagull or anchor plaques. Jason gets up and walks to the front lawn. From there, he turns and looks up at a gable while trying to picture some coastal plaque, then gives the shingled area beside the front door a scrutiny. A plaque could go there, too. The wall lantern softly illuminates those weathered shingles.

"I could be sold on that whole plaque thing," he says, climbing the porch steps and heading to his Adirondack chair. But before he sits, his cell phone starts ringing again inside the house. "I better get it. Could be something for work."

"Okay, babe," Maris says, sipping her wine. "I'll wait here."

⁓

Jason walks down the paneled front hallway toward the kitchen. The jukebox glimmers in its alcove off the living room. And that phone keeps ringing, so he hurries and picks it up from where it's charging on the kitchen counter. He sees, too, who's calling.

"Hey, Shane," Jason says, leaning against the counter. "What's up?"

"Jason." There's a quick breath, then, "Jason, man. Been trying to reach you."

Okay, something's not right. Jason can't miss it in Shane's low voice. "What's going on, guy?" Jason asks him.

"Huh ... I'm not in a good way, man. Pretty fucked up, actually. *Shit.*" Another quick breath as Shane struggles with his words. "Feel like I'm going to lose it."

"Whoa, *whoa*," Jason tells him. "What happened?" he asks, pulling out a stool at the kitchen island. "Everything all right?"

"No."

"You out on the boat?"

"No. I'm home."

There's quiet, then. An alarming quiet coming from Shane. Jason can hear that he's pacing, though. Hears muffled footsteps.

"Just walked in," Shane's voice goes on. "Shit, it's bad. It's bad. It's really bad."

"*What* is, guy? Talk to me."

As Shane falters, there's a faint noise. A scraping—like a kitchen chair being dragged out. *Good*, Jason thinks. *Sit and get the words out.* Problem is, those words aren't making much sense. So Jason presses the phone close to his ear. If Shane just rambles on unimpeded, maybe Jason can pick up on the root of his troubles.

"Again," Shane's saying. "*Again.* Shit, this can't keep happening ... Not supposed to be like this. To *go* like this ... I couldn't change things. Tried, but I just couldn't. Can't change anything in my fuckin' life. I came home afterward—"

"After *what?*" Jason nearly yells.

Because Shane's not stopping now. His nonsensical

talking keeps unrolling. His talk of being trapped there in Maine. Of not knowing what to do. Of doing everything he could earlier but it didn't fucking work. Nothing ever works in his life, no matter how hard he tries. Maybe he'll go out and get something to drink. Everything's falling apart.

"Hang on, Shane!" Jason *does* yell this time. It's the only way to quiet him. "Hang on and get it together, guy," Jason repeats as Maris walks into the kitchen. The dog is at her side as she heads to the table. Jason points to his phone and mouthes, *Shane*.

Maris silently nods and pulls out a chair at that table. Her eyes don't leave Jason's. She slowly sits, riveted to what's unfolding.

"Never mind, Barlow," Shane abruptly tells him. "Just never mind."

Shit, Jason thinks. *Two seconds of motioning to Maris and I've lost Shane's attention.*

"Sorry I bothered you," Shane's saying. His voice is raspy. "Got to get out of here. Right now." There's a new noise as he says it. His chair maybe flipping backward as he stands—*desperate*—in some dark little kitchen in whatever shingled dockside shanty he's living in.

"Oh, no. You stay *right there*," Jason insists, standing now and pacing his own kitchen. He's never heard Shane this down. This shot. "You're not going *anywhere*, you hear me, Shane? Not in that condition. So just go … go get a glass of water, okay? And fucking *sit down*. Because I'm *not* hanging up, damn it." Jason briefly looks to the table at Maris—wide-eyed and glued to his every word. When he walks toward the slider then, the phone is held tight to his

245

ear lest he miss *something* out of Shane. Through the phone, Jason hears the tap running three hundred miles away in Rockport. So he stops right at the slider door and waits.

It's night now. Darkness presses against the glass.

It seems like it's pressing right into Shane's *life*, too.

Some incredible darkness that has him completely unhinged.

Shane finally starts to say something. "*Forget it, Barlow,*" he practically whispers. "*I got to go.*"

"No! No, guy." Jason holds that phone close as though it's keeping Shane tethered to him. "Listen. Hey. Do *not* hang up, Shane. It's going to be all right."

"No," Shane only says. "No, it's not."

"Well, I'm *here*," Jason persists. "And I want to talk to you, man. But you've *got* to stay with me, okay? So slow down, take a breath, and tell me what the *hell* happened."

The beach friends' journey continues in

THE
VISITOR

The next novel in The Seaside Saga from

New York Times Bestselling Author

JOANNE DEMAIO

Also by Joanne DeMaio

Also by Joanne DeMaio

Beach Cottage Series
(In order)
1) The Beach Cottage
2) Back to the Beach Cottage

Standalone Novels
True Blend
Whole Latte Life

The Winter Series
(In order)
1) Snowflakes and Coffee Cakes
2) Snow Deer and Cocoa Cheer
3) Cardinal Cabin
4) First Flurries
5) Eighteen Winters
6) Winter House
—And More Winter Books—

For a complete list of books by *New York Times*
bestselling author Joanne DeMaio, visit:

Joannedemaio.com

About the Author

JOANNE DEMAIO is a *New York Times* and *USA Today* bestselling author of contemporary fiction. The novels of her ongoing and groundbreaking Seaside Saga journey with a group of beach friends, much the way a TV series does, continuing with the same cast of characters from book-to-book. In addition, she writes winter novels set in a quaint New England town. Joanne lives with her family in Connecticut.

For a complete list of books and for news on upcoming releases, visit Joanne's website. She also enjoys hearing from readers on Facebook.

Author Website:
Joannedemaio.com

Facebook:
Facebook.com/JoanneDeMaioAuthor

CPSIA information can be obtained
at www.ICGtesting.com
Printed in the USA
LVHW042051100523
746641LV00003B/320